W. Bridges Birtt

By the Roaring Reuss

Idylls and Stories of the Alps

W. Bridges Birtt

By the Roaring Reuss
Idylls and Stories of the Alps

ISBN/EAN: 9783743417311

Manufactured in Europe, USA, Canada, Australia, Japa

Cover: Foto ©Andreas Hilbeck / pixelio.de

Manufactured and distributed by brebook publishing software (www.brebook.com)

W. Bridges Birtt

By the Roaring Reuss

The Devil's Bridge, over the Reuss.

BY THE ROARING REUSS

IDYLLS AND STORIES OF THE ALPS

BY

W. BRIDGES BIRTT

Author of " The Devil's Triumph";—"Living Sacrifices"
etc., etc.

WITH FOUR FULL-PAGE ILLUSTRATIONS

WESTMINSTER
ARCHIBALD CONSTABLE & Co.
1898

TO

MY DEAR· DAUGHTERS

MAUD AND MARGARET,

IN

REMEMBRANCE OF THEIR

LOVE AND SERVICE.

PREFACE

To me the Urseren valley is a delightful spot; its mountains, meadows and streams are a joy; whilst its people are my friends; and I have only sought in these Idylls to introduce them to others.

I have used a "*raconteur's*" privilege of dealing with dates, events, and places pretty freely; especially has this been so with my use of the Longobard name simply as a family designation. This has been done in order to give these stories a sequence of action and interest.

To those who have helped me with information, or suggested ideas, I tender my grateful thanks; desiring to acknowledge my indebtedness to others for whatsoever aid they may have given.

I hope those who may read these Idylls will find pleasurable profit in doing so; then I shall have realised one of my "heart's desires."

W. B. B.

CONTENTS

I.

MONSIEUR LE CURÉ

MONSIEUR LE CURÉ.

CHAPTER I.

LE CURÉ.

EVERYBODY loved him.

The humble chalets and the greater houses seemed alike the better and purer when he had been there. His presence was like the passing of a sweet, flower-laden breeze through a hot, feverish atmosphere, leaving freshness and fragrance behind it.

He was little of stature, thin and fragile amidst the sturdy, bronzed village folk. He was an old man too, past three-score years and ten; and his steps were growing feebler every year as he tottered along the rough ways which wind about the hills, or by the side of the foaming Reuss as it dashes amongst the boulders and dances under the green banks on its way to the lake of the Four Cantons.

For more than forty years he had been Curé at Hospenthal; first at the church which stands on the hill at the foot of the old Longobard Tower, and then at the quaint little chapel which lies half-hidden amongst the houses lying nearer the main road to Realp. He spoke always of life and its struggles as a man speaks who has suffered keenly, but who has found his way out of the storms and bitterness into the sweetness and peace of victory.

He knew far more about the feelings and the experiences of these simple villagers than anybody else, and the histories of their hard toils, keen struggles and secret hopes were as the pages of an open book to him. The old people revered him, the younger ones trusted him, whilst the children loved to cluster about him, and little Pierre Meyer said, that he "was like an old angel who had lost his wings."

Wherever sickness or sorrow came amongst
the village folk there was found the Curé
to cheer and comfort; and often as he toiled
to the far-off home of some troubled family
in the higher valleys, he was compelled to
take refuge in rough chalets or wayside
shelters, and was sometimes kept there for
days by the fierceness of the storms.

Winter and summer the Curé was ready
to pray with his people and bless them
before they went to their daily toil; and the
working-day began early with these dwellers in this village by the roaring Reuss.
At four o'clock on summer mornings when
the Ursuren valley was sweet and fresh
with the cool breeze as it blew down from
snow-clad heights, and half an hour later
on winter mornings, when the freshness
had become a biting frost and the valley
was covered with snow many feet deep,
the aged Curé was ready in the little chapel
to offer the early Mass.

At the close of the service one wild
morning in October, the Curé saw a stout,

comfortably clad woman waiting until the other worshippers had passed out. He knew she was anxious to speak to him, and so walked slowly towards her.

"Why, is that you, Jeanne?" he asked in surprise, when he recognised her as he came nearer, for his sight was growing dim.

"Yes, Father, it is."

"Are you all well?"

"Yes, we are all well; but I'm troubled in my mind."

"Ah, what troubles you, my daughter? I thought you had had a good season and the cattle had all done well and that you were prosperous and happy."

"That is so, Father, but I am troubled about somebody else; and I don't know whether I ought to say anything about it."

"Well, what is it?"

"Some days ago a lady came from Altdorf and wished to stop with us for a few weeks. She is growing old and feeble, but one can easily tell she is a real lady of France."

"It is very late in the season for a visitor to come to the village, Jeanne."

"I told her so, and pointed out the difficulties to her; but she only smiled and said she would pay me liberally if I would receive her; and I consented."

"Then what is your trouble, Jeanne?"

"Well, she has not left the house since she entered it, and all day long whenever I pass her chamber I can hear her sighing and sobbing as only a heart-broken woman *can* sob; and it troubles me, Father, day and night."

"Has she said anything to you about herself or her trouble?"

"Not a word. She only smiles and speaks pleasantly about the village and the mountains when I am in her room."

"Ah," said the Curé, as he rubbed his chin thoughtfully; "I will try and call to-day, or to-morrow, and perhaps she will see me and I may be of help to her."

He little thought what it all meant to him.

CHAPTER II.

THE LITTLE CHAPEL.

THE house where the Curé lived adjoins the little chapel where for so many years he ministered. It is a quaint, well-kept building, with an aisle leading from the entrance straight up to the altar rails. On either side of the aisle there is a row of rough, unstained pine seats, by no means suggestive of bodily comfort in worship. The entrance is covered with a large square porch supported by strong pillars springing from a low, rough, stone balustrade which surrounds three sides of the porch and serves as a seat for those who wish to rest or talk. On each side of the door there is a small square opening filled with iron grating and having wooden shutters inside, so that when these are open those in the porch can have an uninterrupted view of the interior.

Long years before, when the Ursuren valley was more sparsely inhabited and opportunities of religious service were few and distant, this chapel had been built and endowed by a wealthy family at that time resident or interested in the village. These have all passed away, but the results of their thoughtfulness and charity still remain for the comfort and help of others.

On the left side of the altar as you stand looking towards it, and about ten feet from the floor, there is a little semi-gothic oriel window, but unglazed, and any worshipper sitting there can hear and see all that passes in the chapel without being noticed. It opens into a little chamber in the Curé's house and might have been designed for midnight vigils, or for the use of some invalid.

In the gathering dusk of that October day the Curé entered the chamber, and looking down from the oriel window, he saw a woman kneeling near one of the side benches. This was no uncommon thing for him to see, for often in the twilight the villagers would turn in for restful quiet and to say an evening prayer. As he stood, however, he heard a burst of sobbing as from a heavily burdened heart. He thought it might be the French lady of whom Jeanne had spoken, and he decided to go and speak to her. He descended the narrow staircase and entered the chapel, treading so softly that she did not hear him coming and was only aware of his presence when he spoke. She gave a little start, and drew herself up, and as she did so he saw she was thickly veiled.

"Madame, I beg you to pardon my intrusion, but as I am Curé here, I should like to say that I am at your service."

"I thank you very sincerely, Monsieur." And the voice was the voice of a refined gentlewoman.

The Curé started and looked round as though some long-lost melody had stolen into the place.

"Perhaps you are in trouble and I may be able to give you advice or comfort."

Through her thick veil and in the dim light of the chapel she could only see indistinctly; yet as she gazed for a few moments on his pale and aged face she thought it had the sweetness of an angel's.

"Yes, Monsieur, I am troubled, but I know of nothing which can comfort me this side the grave."

Again he started at the sound of the voice as though it brought back some painful memory, but he put down his foot firmly and waved his hand as if waving the thought away.

"Will you not confide in me, Madame? And if I can, I will help you."

"Monsieur, I have never told my care to mortal yet, but there is something within impelling me to tell my story to you in this lonely mountain spot. I know not what it is, but I feel I cannot resist the impulse."

"I am ready to listen, Madame."

"Long, long years ago I was one of the happiest, merriest maidens in the whole of

Normandy. My parents lived in a quiet village not far from the banks of the Seine, and I was their only child, caressed and petted by all. I was betrothed to one of the purest, best men I have ever known, a young *avocat* from Rouen, named Alphonse Regnier."

The Curé was startled, and clutched the back of the seat near him.

"About this time I met a handsome young lieutenant who was visiting at a house in the village. There was everything about him to wile and charm a village girl. He was constantly seeking my society, and fascinated me with his manners and flattering compliments. At length he persuaded me to meet him clandestinely in Paris and marry him. At first I shrunk horrified from such a suggestion, but he quieted all my scruples and beguiled me into consenting. Before long I found I had married one of the greatest gamesters and libertines in Paris. What I suffered at his hands no creature but myself ever knew, and the

misery was made tenfold more awful by
the reproaches of my conscience as I remembered the goodness and tenderness of
Alphonse. I resolved that I would bear
my wretchedness alone and that none of
my kindred should ever know of my whereabouts if I could help it; but I learned that
my sainted father and mother both died
broken-hearted on account of my folly and
wrong. After years of degradation and woe,
my husband shot himself in my presence
and fell dead at my feet.

"I was left a widow with one child, a
bright, beautiful boy, on whom I lavished
my whole affection. I spared nothing if it
made him happier or fitted him better for
life and society; but as he grew up, I saw
many of his father's traits of character re-
produced in him, and I shuddered as on the
brink of a yawning, black abyss. At a
suitable age he became an officer in the
same regiment to which his father had
belonged and I saw that the same fascination of manner was causing him to lead

others from virtue to vice, from honour to shame. I poured out my soul in entreaties to him, and he smiled and promised better things; but, alas! the unfaithfulness which had ruined the father cursed also the life of the son. At length, one wild, stormy winter's night he was brought home to me, cold, and dead; stabbed to the heart by the lover of a maiden he had wronged. Then it seemed to me that all things were given over to the power of the devil and the rule of wrong, and in my lonely misery I could only lie and cry, 'My God, my God, why hast Thou forsaken me?'

"Months elapsed before I rallied from the awful blow, and then my heart turned as a child's to the quiet Normandy village by the Seine; and I longed to know something about the old home and the man I had so shamefully abandoned, but never ceased to love. But I could learn nothing about him, only that in his disappointment and wretchedness he had sacrificed all prospects of earthly prosperity and entered into a distant monastery. It is forty-five years since I looked on his face the last time in my father's house, and perhaps if I could see it now it might be as changed as my own, and I should hardly know it; but I feel that if I could see it again and hear him say he had forgiven me, I could die in thankfulness and peace."

The Curé still stood clutching the old pine seat, but he was trembling like a storm-swept tree. At length he moved nearer the centre of the aisle, still clinging to the bench, and gazed steadfastly at her, saying softly in a voice of indescribable pathos—

"Josephine, Josephine."

She threw back her dark veil, and gave one quick, eager look into his eyes; then uttering a cry which filled the little sanctuary and went out into the dark nightfall, she fell on her knees on the floor and clasped her hands as in an agony.

The Curé bent forward, gently touching her quivering and clenched hands.

"Yes, Josephine, thou hast thy wish. Thou

seest me again, but old, bent and broken; the vows of forty years are upon me, during which I have been trying to forget thee and my love for thee, in devotion to Christ and in my service to my poor people in these wild and lonely hills. I have suffered truly, but, thank God, the baptism is past."

"Oh! Alphonse, Alphonse, listen to my plea, and let me hear you say you forgive me, and I shall be content to suffer or to die."

A sweet smile lit up the furrowed face as, turning and pointing to a figure of the crucified Christ hanging near, he said, " As truly as I hope to be forgiven by Him who died on the Cross, so truly have I long ago forgiven thee, Josephine. Thou hast suffered bitterly, the cross thou hast carried has been rough and heavy, and it cannot be laid down entirely whilst life shall last; but I will pray for thee and perchance thou wilt find it grow lighter, and the hands of the Crucified will bear it for thee. I am glad I have looked once again on thy face, and heard again the voice I loved to hear in the old home in Normandy; but leave me now to my awakened memories and to my prayers. Adieu, Josephine; go in peace."

So out into the darkness which was only the harbinger of the light, slowly crept the stricken yet comforted woman.

CHAPTER III.

As the door closed upon the retreating form of Josephine, the Curé shut the shutters which covered the open grilles, and walking slowly and feebly up the aisle to the foot of the altar, he fell on his knees on the cold, hard, stone floor.

The chapel was full of deep shadows cast by the one tiny lamp which burned constantly in front of the altar. Not a sound came from the village where the people had settled down to their evening work in the early October night; only a faint humming sound from the distant rushing Reuss crept into the building, as when a gentle breeze rambles amongst the branches of a pine forest on the hills.

With this soft music of the waters there mingled the sounds of frequent sobs and murmured prayers, at intervals.

"Oh God, Thou knowest I am old and feeble and spent, and the wounds I thought had healed for ever have been opened and probed to their depths. Forgive me, Oh my God, forgive me every sin of thought or desire, and uphold me, for I am like a bruised reed in a tempest. Give me the victory and the perfect peace. Let no harm come to my children here through wrong in me."

Through the long hours the silence now and again throbbed with the old man's sighs and prayers; still he knelt on, keeping his vigil of sorrow and love.

Gradually his head bent lower and lower until his brow touched the cold stone altar-step above him, and not a sound broke the awful stillness save the distant murmur of the rushing stream.

When the villagers came for the early morning service they found him still kneeling on the cold floor. They waited for him to rise and robe for the service, and when he did so and turned his face towards them,

a sense of awe fell upon all; for as they
"looked steadfastly on him, they saw his
face as it had been the face of an angel."

The Curé had found the restfulness of
victory and peace. The night vigil of sorrow
had ended in the morning dawn of joy.
He had stood in the Eternal Light, and the
radiance and beauty were upon him still.

When the next winter's snows covered
the valley the Curé passed suddenly and
peacefully away. He was found dead, kneeling on the altar steps in the little church
he loved so well; a smile of sweet content
lingering on his worn and aged face.

When they laid him to rest in the little
church-yard overlooking the roaring Reuss,
the sorrowful peasants from all parts of the
valley gathered to the ceremony; but no
sadder mourner was there than an old and
feeble woman thickly veiled in black and
leaning on the arm of the weeping Jeanne.

II.

THE OLD TOWER

II.

THE OLD TOWER.

CHAPTER I.

THE TOWER STEPS.

At the upper end of the village of Hospenthal stands the old " Longobard Tower". Many generations ago, on a rugged mound of granite rock standing about two hundred feet above the winding street, the Longobards had built themselves a lofty, square tower of five stories high. Its walls at the base are some six feet in thickness, whilst on the upper stories they are very little less.

Below roars the river Reuss, its waters tossed and foamed by contact with the fragments of rock which the storms and avalanches have sent bounding from the heights, and whose ceaseless rush fills the valley with its monotonous music.

The Tower dominates the valley on all sides, and it would have been no easy task in those far-off days to scale and take it. It had been built as a watch-tower for the valley, so that from its loopholes the approach of friend or foe could be easily seen. There was no entrance to it from the exterior, it could only be entered by a rough, underground passage which led from the dwelling of the barons lower down at the foot of the rock, and opened on to the dark ground floor of the massive structure.

High up on the south side where the rock rises almost perpendicularly, so that the building seems as though it were only the rock upheaving itself towards the deep blue sky, there is an opening like a doorway, but it is placed so high in the wall that it could never have been an ordinary entrance to the building, though it may have been used for the purpose of light and of hoisting up those things which could not be taken through the small and confined underground passage.

Far below stand the houses of the village, some of them rough old chalets turning brown and red, like beings bronzed by fierce storms and suns. Humble homes where the same passions rage and the same sorrows sob as in the homes of great and crowded cities.

From the east side of the Tower you have a magnificent view over Andermatt, the entrance to the gorge where the Devil's Bridge spans the turbulent Reuss, and of the dark, rugged heights which guard the Oberalp Pass. On the west side the eye travels up the valley towards the Furka, whilst far away the route seems blocked by the snow-covered Muttenhorn. On the south the valley is shut in by the St. Gothard mountain group, and on the north by the chain which leads on to the wild and lofty Galenstock.

It is a fair and lovely scene, and gazed on in the warm summer sunlight, when the

green meadows of the valley are thickly
dotted with the bluest of blue forget-me-
nots, and here and there is seen the deep,
dark blue of the gentians, whilst patches
of the pale yellow "bouton-d'or" are
nodding at the touch of the cool northerly
breeze, and all is watched over by the silent
snowy heights; it is a scene which imprints
itself on the memory never to be effaced.

On just such a day when the sun was
casting the long shadows of the Tower on
the rough steps which led down to the
church, a maiden was sitting near the top
of them, with a lap full of wild flowers
which she was arranging in a tasteful bouquet,
and softly humming over an old mountain
melody.

Suddenly she heard footsteps close behind
her, and looking up, saw a tall, bronzed
young man with keen, dark eyes full of
slumbering passion-fire, looking eagerly at
her. His dress was better than that of the
general villagers and suggested that he
occupied a superior social position.

"Good morning, Alice," he said, as he raised his cap. "I am delighted to meet you here this morning, because it is so long since I had an opportunity of speaking to you."

She took no notice, only went on arranging her flowers.

"You do not seem pleased to see me, evidently."

Still she gave no heed to him, but went on sorting and placing her flowers.

"Alice, will you listen to me? You know I love you above all others, and I shall never be content until you accept me."

"I have told you, Monsieur, again and again, I do not and cannot respond to your feeling. And I think it is unworthy of you to persecute me with your attentions."

"But you will care for me some day, Alice."

"Never."

"Well, I shall wait patiently."

"It will be useless; besides I am already betrothed, and my wedding day is near."

"What? Are you going to marry that base-born fool, André Keller?"

"Yes, I am; and I am proud of it. You know that André Keller is one of the bravest, kindest men in the valley. You know it, but your pride won't allow you to own it. Your selfishness makes you unjust; and besides you have no right to speak of him in that way to me." And she arose, and drew herself up haughtily.

"Bah! What rubbish!" And he laughed aloud in sheer scorn.

"You may laugh, Monsieur, but that will make no difference."

"Won't it? You will see. He shall *never* be your husband." And his fierce eyes flashed like a demon's.

"Jean de Longobard, you are mean, spiteful and jealous; you are cruel—cruel as the grave. If one spark of honour remains in you as the last of your race, retract your words and leave me."

"*Retract* them? A Longobard never does that. *Retract* them? No. I will *repeat* them, and swear by yonder eternal peaks that he shall not have you."

"He clenched his teeth and raised his hand whilst he hissed, rather than uttered, the words; and with eyes blazing with fury he bounded wildly down the rough steps.

Alice trembled as she saw him go, for she knew well his fierce ungovernable passion, but hope filled her spirit and brought calm and peace in its train; and knowing that André would be at Milan for some weeks she trusted that the vehemence of Jean de Longobard's passion would die away, and all would be well. So, gathering up her flowers which had fallen on the grass during the interview, she went slowly down into the village.

CHAPTER II.

THE OLD HOME.

ALICE MÜLLER was a typical Swiss maiden, lithe and graceful, fair of skin, with rich masses of brown hair, and eyes as blue as the forget-me-nots of the valley. Her home was at Wassen, a picturesque village not far from Göschenen. Much of her time was spent with a widowed aunt at Hospenthal: and here she first met with André Keller, the village smith. Here too she met with Jean de Longobard, who had been smitten with her charms the first time he saw her, and never lost any opportunity which presented itself of urging his attentions upon her, although she persistently refused them and avoided him as often as she possibly could.

On the southern side of the rocky mound on which the tower stands, and close to its foot, is a quaint old stone house; it is almost buried amongst a group of brown wooden chalets, yet it is still suggestive of strength and importance.

On the ground floor of this house and facing towards the street, are the large square doors which lead to the common store-house for fuel and implements, and also a low archway fitted with strong doors and bars. On either side of the doorways a square opening serving as a window, is strongly protected with a coarse, iron grille fixed to the walls. The house has a high-pitched gabled front, with three little windows on each of the chief floors, and one in the sharp gable. The house stretches back to the rock where it is level with the second floor, and is almost touched by the long, sloping roof. On the side towards Andermatt there is a broad, rough, covered stairway leading to the dwelling rooms, and which is indeed the chief entrance to the old house.

Doubtless the house and its offices cover-ed greater space in the distant days when the Longobards were a power in Urseren, and in all probability the surrounding chalets only crept up to it years after the decay of their power and influence. Indeed it is not impossible that the present house, old as it is, was one built on the site of an older and much more important building.

This was the dwelling of Jean de Longobard, the last of his race, whose fortunes, like his house, were stamped with the impress of weakness and decay.

He had often been persuaded to leave it, but on this point he was immovable. He *only* knew of the entrance to the subterraneous passage which connected the house with the tower, and though now it is a roofless and dismantled ruin with an opening knocked roughly through the base of its thick eastern wall in order to gain admission to it, it was in his days a strong and secure retreat; which to a man of his solitary habits and moody, passionate nature would be accounted a privilege to possess. So he lived on at the old home with no companionship save that of a great St. Bernard dog and an aged, wrinkled woman who had been his nurse in childhood and who because of her long and faithful service had become his confidante and adviser in all things.

In the evening of the day on which he had encountered Alice by the Tower, he was sitting in an antique carved oak chair by one of the three windows which lighted the only sitting-room of the house, and gazing moodily through the open window on the quiet street of the village. His great dog lay at his feet, looking up with a wondering gaze into his master's face, not understanding why he had no kind word for him; and so gently touching him now and again with his great paw to attract his notice. Presently his hand was placed on the dog's head, as he quietly said, "My faithful lover, dear old Carlo."

The dog raised himself, and stretching up, fondly licked his master's swarthy face.

The door of the room was opened and the old servant came in with an ancient bronze lamp.

"You see I am still here, Anna, quietly thinking."

"It seems to me you do too much of that every day."

"Ah well; I cannot help it. You know it has been my habit all my life. I am afraid I like to sit alone and brood."

"There is no doubt of it."

"Anna, I met Alice Müller to-day."

"Well, and what said she?"

"She refused me again, and told me she was betrothed to André Keller."

"The little minx. She does not know what is best for her. Take my advice, Monsieur Jean, forget her and let her see you do not care for her."

"Anna, I *cannot*." And he sprang up from his chair with a sudden bound. "She is part of my life. But André Keller shall never have her."

Anna saw his flashing eyes and set mouth, and a sharp anguish smote her heart, for she knew him well.

CHAPTER III.

THE DEVIL'S BRIDGE.

THE October snows had begun to fall on the heights around Hospenthal; and a fire was burning in the stove of Jean de Longobard's sitting-room. Already the autumn day was beginning to fade, as Anna brought in coffee for her master.

He drank it in feverish haste, and rising, said with a smile that seemed diabolical in its malice, "This is André Keller's wedding day. Won't you wish him joy, Anna?" And with a glance of hatred which lit up his face as with a flashing flame of hell, he opened the door and went hurriedly down the stone steps, bidding Carlo stop behind.

After he had gone Anna remembered seeing a pistol stuck in his leather belt, and she sat down in the nearest seat, trembling with excitement and expectation of disaster.

Almost leaping down the steps, Jean de Longobard turned swiftly to the left and took the road to Andermatt, but avoided as much of the village as he could by passing close by the church and coming out near where the rough path climbs up to the Oberalp; he then walked swiftly on towards the place where the Reuss is crossed by the well-known Devil's Bridge.

Here the rocks rise almost perpendicularly to an enormous height, and are slashed and seamed and smoothed by the fearful storms and avalanches which are found here; whilst the utter absence of vegetation from their huge granite slopes gives them a wilder form and casts about them a greater spirit of awe.

The river roars as with a thunder tone a hundred feet below the roadway, and is dashed, foaming in its curving bed, over huge boulders. As it falls into a deep pool from the higher rock it seems to make a seething, boiling cauldron, and its spray is floated like a damp mist far above the Bridge; and the turbulent river goes roaring on down into the valley, with a force nothing can resist.

Even in the sunshine the place is full of awfulness and fear, but when the last rays of the sun have left the mountain tops and the evening shadows creep over the whole, it is one of the weirdest spots man can find, full of glooms and suggestive of terror.

Those who would come from Wassen to Hospenthal must pass through this gorge and over the Devil's Bridge. The road after winding up by long zig-zags from the valley to this spot, turns sharply round a rock and brings one suddenly in full view of the deep chasm spanned by the Bridge.

Just where the road turns round the projecting rock and on the side towards the Bridge, there is a high perpendicular fissure in its surface in which a man can stand, and in the shadows of evening not be seen by any person coming up from the valley. Without even a glance at the wild torrent of waters sweeping along below him, and only looking keenly round to see if he were watched, Jean de Longobard stepped quickly across the Bridge and stood in this fissure, leaning his back against the rock.

At the church on the knoll at Wassen, André Keller and Alice Müller had been made that day husband and wife, and according to the custom, were returning home to Hospenthal in one of the long, narrow waggons of the district, he driving and she seated in the vehicle surrounded by various articles of housekeeping which had been the gifts of their kinsfolk and friends.

Jean de Longobard's intimate knowledge of the ways and customs of the district enabled him to judge pretty accurately the time at which they would reach the Bridge; so he stood patiently waiting in his jealous madness their arrival on the scene. In a short time he heard the sound of approach-

"The church on the knoll at Wassen."

ing voices, and he crept cautiously to the edge of the rock and gazed down the road; he saw it was André driving and he slunk back to his hiding-place. He had hardly set himself firmly in the dark shadow of the fissure, when he heard a deep, rushing sound, high up in the still air on the lonely heights some distance behind him. His heart seemed to stand still, and a great sweat of fear stood on his brow. He knew too well what it was, a great avalanche had started on its course into the valley. In a few seconds it fell with an awful, thundering thud on the road behind the rock, bounding over the precipice and carrying all before it into the river, and sending its waters hissing all around. One wild, piercing scream, never to be forgotten by him who heard it, rang through the gorge, and then all was hushed, save for the tumult of the waters.

The avalanche had killed André and Alice and swept them with the horse and waggon into the boiling stream below.

Jean de Longobard stood a moment dazed and paralysed, then as though seized with a panic of fear and horror, he flung the pistol which he held in his hand into the ravine, and rushing across the Bridge, he ran, like one pursued by demons, until he reached the village of Hospenthal.

CHAPTER IV.

THE GORGE.

A FEW hundred yards from the old Tower, and on the edge of the upper valley leading to the summit of the St. Gothard Pass, the Reuss flows through a small, but deep and picturesque gorge. This gorge is reached by a narrow footway roughly cut in the face of the shaly rocks, and on a level with the stream. The path leads to a tiny piece of shingly shore lying in a hollow in the hill side.

Just above, the river turns a sharp corner and comes tumbling down in dancing white cascades. The bed is filled with immense boulders, which stand like great bulwarks in the midst of the stream, defying its onward progress; but the river rushes on, now leaping over some and breaking into fresh sparkling foam; now wildly beating itself against others in impotent rage, and gliding round their base to toss itself into the angry stream below. The sides of the steeps which shut it in are green to the water's edge, and make a lovely setting for the white foam of the stream

As you sit on the tiny shingle shore, you see on your right, some old chalets and the square old Tower; whilst high above these stand the great silent rocks with their caps of snow. On your left, through a narrow opening, you get a peep at one of the mighty hills which stand as sentinels, guarding the road to the summit of the Pass.

When the sun shines down into the hollow, making the waters flash and shimmer like a stream composed of myriads of crystals, and the green banks smile with verdant beauty, it might be the trysting-place of the elves and fairies; but when the sun has gone down behind the hills and the stars peep out on the purple night, the spot is wild, weird and uncanny. The elves have gone, and a host of the spirits of evil may have taken their place. The noise of the waters seems deafening and might be only the howls of the evil host which people it.

In this wild, lonely spot sat Jean de Longobard on that awful October night. Hour after hour he sat on in darkness, the commotion of the waters being only a figure of the wilder tempest of feeling which surged through his soul.

"Yes, yes," he moaned aloud; "I am that despicable creature—a murderer and a coward. I went there to commit murder, it was the purpose of my heart; I had vowed that André Keller should not have Alice, and I meant to keep my vow; and only the fall of the avalanche prevented it. The horrible thing is branded on my soul,—a murderer. I must fly. I cannot look these village folk in the face again. O God, save me from myself." And he fell prostrate in his conscience-stricken agony on the shingly shore; his wailing cry lost in the roar of the river.

The day was breaking when he entered his house, and found that Anna had been wearily waiting for his return through the long night. The faithful servant was startled at his pale, haggard face, and pushed a chair forward for him to sit in. He fell wearily into it, and Carlo sprang up to lick his face.

"Poor old dog. A nobler creature than thy master; always ready to save a life and not destroy it. Poor old dog." And his hand rested fondly on his head.

"Anna, say no word about it, but André and Alice are both dead."

Anna placed her hand on her lips to still the scream which escaped from them.

"Yes, both dead. Killed, Anna; but not by me."

She gave a great sigh of relief and burst into tears.

"I did not kill them, but I went to the Devil's Bridge intending to shoot André as he came round the rock; but before they reached me an avalanche fell and swept

them into the chasm. Oh! that awful shriek
from Alice, how it pierced my brain. I
shall never get it out of my ears till I die.
Anna," he said after a pause, "I am a
murderer."

"No, no, Master, not that," she said
piteously.

"Yes, Anna, it is true. I had it in my
heart. I intended to kill André; and then
when the avalanche fell I fled like a conscience-stricken coward."

"Take some rest, Master; and you will
feel better."

"No. I have spent the night in the
gorge here, and I have decided what to
do. I shall quit Hospenthal to-night for
ever."

"O, Monsieur Jean, don't do anything
so rash and hasty."

"Anna," he said firmly, "I have made
up my mind. Put a few needful things
into my old knapsack during the day, and
when the evening falls I and Carlo will
start for Italy. I shall leave you in charge

here as long as you live, and I will show you the secret entrance to the Tower before I go. It may be useful to you. And if ever any poor hunted creature asks shelter and refuge from you, give it to him in the security of the old Tower, in memory of me and of my bitter repentance."

She knew his determined spirit and strong will too well to try to oppose them, so she uttered no word as she bowed her head on the old oak table.

When the evening came he stood at the door, equipped for his walk, with Carlo at his side. He was calm and firm, but the fierce fire had died out of his eyes, and a soft, tender light filled them. He bent down, and taking Anna's white head between his hands he kissed her again and again on her time-wrinkled brow.

"Adieu, Anna—Adieu, my faithful and life-long friend."

The old servant's heart was too full for words; she could not speak.

Then giving one lingering look round

the room, Jean de Longobard went silently down into the village street, self-exiled from the home of his race.

Anna watched him as long as she could, then going into the house, she closed and fastened the door on her loneliness, and spent the night in a sorrowful vigil in her master's old oak chair.

III.

BROTHER ANTONIO

.

4

III.

BROTHER ANTONIO.

CHAPTER I.

THE HOSPICE.

THE Hospice of St. Gothard stands in a magnificent loneliness of granite and wild water. The chalets are left far below, the firs and pines have vanished, and the few wild flowers found there seem to have a difficulty in finding a place in which to grow. All about great boulders and splintered rocks, and above, the white peaks of the mountains. It is just a birth-place of tempests and a cradle of storms.

The Hospice stands a little below the top of the Pass, near the "eternal lakes" from which the rivers Ticino and the Reuss flow. It is the fourth in a succession of shelters which have crowned this wild and desolate region with their beneficent help and succour since the beginning of the fourteenth century, and which have a splendid record of rescue and refuge through all the long years; but though old and discarded now, the present building is nevertheless replete with interesting memories, and fancy still peoples the spot with the brown-clad Capuchin monks, and groups of St. Bernard dogs. The rocks seem the eternal monuments reared to the self-denial, charity and devotion of these men.

The building is a plain, oblong structure of the most meagre and unpretending description, its ground floor of stone and its upper stories covered with wood. A tiny bayed window on the first floor immediately to the right above the entrance door, marks the room occupied by the Prior of the little establishment. The door opens on to a stone passage, on the left of which is a stone staircase leading to the chief rooms, all of which are lined with wood blackened and browned by age.

At the foot of the stairs the stone passage leads into the chapel, a long, dim chamber with an arched roof. The altar stands in a semicircular recess at the east end, lighted by a little window at each side. In the west end is placed another small window, below which is a gallery, entered from the first floor, and where the bell is rung which hangs in the stone turret above the roof of the chapel. This bell is rung still at certain hours to warn the herdsmen and summon them homewards, and the tones seem peculiarly solemn as they peal out over the lonely scene.

A low stone terrace or raised path extends the length of the front, and on the left is the Morgue, a large, low, octagonal building with a wooden shingle roof. Here were placed to await identification, the bodies of those who perished in the snows, or by the avalanches. In front, the rough ground leads to the edge of the precipice looking down into Val Tremola. To the left are the heights of the Pizzo Centrale

and Monte Prosa; to the right, the steep
Fibbia and other peaks of the great St.
Gothard group, whose rents and seams
are filled with snow even in the summer time.

In the afternoon of a clear September
day two monks were standing at the door
of the Hospice, looking out towards the
road which comes up from Airolo. There
was an unusual seriousness marking their
manner and speech, as they stroked the
heads of two St. Bernard dogs which stood
near them.

"It is sad to think of the losses we have
sustained in our numbers during the past
year; we must have some reinforcements
before the winter, otherwise we shall not
be able to cope with the storms and difficulties of the season."

So spake the older of the two monks
and the Prior of the House. The younger
monk was only a recent addition to the
ranks of the Hospice.

"What help do you think needful, Father,
under the circumstances?"

"We cannot do with less than two extra lay helpers and another brother of our order."

"Have you laid the matter before the Chapter at Milan?"

"Most surely I have, my son. I sent a special messenger to acquaint them with our position, and an answer was returned by the courier that the thing should be laid before the Chapter as soon as possible. I know that it is not easy to arrange it, for it is not every brother who is fitted to bear the fatigues and severity of this terrible spot for the prescribed period, during which the brethren who come must remain here. Indeed the dwelling in our sunny Italy only increases the difficulty, by rendering men less fit for the rigours and hardships of this Pass, where nearly eight months out of the twelve are wild and wintry. However, the Abbot will assuredly send us the best assistance he can."

Whilst they were talking, a tall, spare man clad in the Capuchin garb was seen coming over the brow of the hill in front of them. He carried a strong alpen-stock, and by his side walked a magnificent specimen of a St. Bernard hound.

"Verily," said the Prior, who first caught sight of him, "this must be one of our brethren from Milan."

The new comer saluted the Prior and presented a letter to him, which he read hastily and then carefully folded away.

"Ah," said he, "the Abbot tells me that certain brethren are appointed to help us, and that you are sent on in advance to bring us the tidings and to serve in our Hospice, bearing us company in our work of charity here. He speaks well of your self-denying devotion, and indeed there is much need of it in this trying position. We welcome you heartily, Brother Antonio,— for such I gather is your name—to our little fraternity."

The stranger only bowed his head and smiled.

Meantime the Hospice dogs had been

closely examining the hound which had come with Brother Antonio, at first some-what resenting his introduction amongst them; but apparently soon recognising his kinship and power, they received him with silent dignity and allowed him to follow his master into the Hospice without further protest.

CHAPTER II.

BROTHER Antonio moved about like a man whose soul was burdened with some sore trial. He attended readily to all the duties which were laid upon him, but went about them with a chastened and quiet spirit, like a man who "goes softly" after some great conflict or sorrow. He shrank from no peril, and only smiled if in a wild storm he was called out to succour some belated traveller.

In the Hospice no austerities were practised, they lived as well as circumstances would allow, for it was necessary that everything should be done to keep up their physical strength for the trying duties they had to perform; but Brother Antonio disregarded all these things, and everything that savoured of comfort or luxury was cut off from his life; his self-denial was of the most

rigorous kind. He grew thinner each passing week, and his dark eyes shone with a
marvellous lustre in his emaciated face; yet
he showed no diminution of activity. To
the Prior's expostulations he listened patiently, but begged to be allowed to follow his
own course for " conscience' sake."

Often when the hour for retiring rang,
he quietly passed into the cold, damp chapel
and spent the night in prayer on the hard
stone pavement; but he was always ready
to take his share of the earliest morning
duties. His brethren in the Hospice soon
began to feel that he moved in a region
of spiritual elevation of which they knew
but little; but his separate inner life as it
touched and influenced his daily actions
awoke no distrust nor jealousy, because it
was so natural and unostentatious.

The winter was passing by without any
very extraordinary difficulties or dangers.
Christmas had come and gone, with its
pleasant Bethlehem memories peacefully
celebrated by the dwellers and guests in

the Hospice; and the brethren were con-
gratulating themselves on their escape from
unusual perils, when, at the close of January
a terrible storm changed the whole aspect
of things in the Hospice.

For some days the Pass had been wrapped in a dense, dark mist, almost turning
day into night. When this lifted, snow
began to fall afresh, heaping itself up on
that which had already fallen until it seemed
as though the Hospice itself would be
blotted out of sight, or destroyed by an
avalanche like its forerunner in 1779. A
furious wind arose which drove the soft
snow into large drifts of twenty and thirty
feet deep, and as it howled and hurled
itself against the hills only to be beaten
back by their granite bulwarks, it went shrieking on over the Pass like a host of raging
spirits, seizing the Hospice in its grip and
shaking it like a reed in the fury of its wrath.

When the storm was spent the monks
began to make preparations to leave the
house in quest of any travellers who might

have been lost in the snow. One of the
first to start on this difficult errand was
Brother Antonio, who, calling his hound to
him, and accompanied by a lay brother,
succeeded at great risk in getting near the
track by which travellers passed to and fro.
The danger was great, and calamities during
such seasons were frequent and terrible;
rescuers and rescued sometimes perishing
together within sight of the friendly Hospice.
The previous winter two of the monks and
three travellers together with two dogs, had
perished in the fall of an avalanche.

It is marvellous what power and sagacity
these dogs have; trained to their work
they rarely ever fail in scenting the lost
under the snow and getting them out; and
one dog has been known to save more
than fifteen lives.

Brother Antonio had reached the spot
where the road passes between the two
lakes when the hound began excitedly
scenting the snow around him. He soon
came to a stand-still and began to paw

the snow aside; in a short time the form
of a man clad as a peasant was discovered. His face was turned towards
the ground, whilst his arm was round the
form of a little child who was carefully
wrapped in the goat-skin cape which the
man had taken off himself for the protection
of his little lad. The monk saw that the
peasant was dead—frozen to death, and
turned his attention to the child who was
asleep, but still warm. He put him into
the arms of the lay brother and bade him
take him at once to the shelter and warmth
of the Hospice, where he soon rallied and
did well. Later, the father's body was taken
to the Morgue. In a lonely Alpine Pass,
or in a busy English town, it is still true
that "a father pitieth his children". It is the
same untold power of love; the fatherhood or
motherhood sacrifices itself for the children.

Left alone, Brother Antonio thought he
heard sounds which indicated other travellers in peril, and he pushed on in order to
help them; but he found none. His own

strength was giving way; he felt he could go no further, and in his utter weakness, sat down in the shadow of a rock which overhung the narrow way where it began its last ascent from Hospenthal to the summit of the Pass. It was snowing again heavily, and the blinding flakes of snow bewildered him and made the possibilities of return utterly impracticable to him in his weak and exhausted condition. The dog nestled close up to him, and as he rested his nose on the brother's knee, seemed to realise all the danger and hopelessness of their position; and after looking keenly into the face of the monk, licked his hand and then gave one long, piercing howl, which seemed to fill the gorge with shrieking echoes and ghostly moans.

Brother Antonio put out his cold, numbed hand and placed it on the head of the dog.

"Poor old fellow! My loyal friend. *Sauve-toi.*"

The noble creature only crept closer to his master, and watched him as wistfully and keenly as he could in the gathering darkness.

CHAPTER III.

THE twin Angels of Death and Sleep were wandering over the Alpine valleys in the gathering mists and snows of the winter night, and came near the weary, suffering Brother Antonio.

Then said Sleep as he beheld him, "This poor, worn traveller is weary and sad. The storms have been too fierce for him, the pains of life have filled his eyes with tears; I will close them with my touch of forgetfulness." And as he touched him the pains and struggles were as nothing to him, for they were shut out from his feeling by the benevolent gift of the good Spirit of Sleep.

The twin brother Death gazed upon it with sadness and silent awe.

"Why thy sad look of silence, my brother?" demanded the Spirit of Sleep.

"Are we not brothers?" asked the Angel of Death. "And yet how different our work, and how opposite the way in which men think of us. When thou hast touched men they fall into the silence of sweet forgetfulness; but in hamlet and town, in the valleys and on the hills men come forth from the shadows of sleep at the day-dawn into the gladness of renewed life and work, and they bless thee for the gentle ministries of thy touch. When I touch men they also fall into forgetfulness, but my coming only awakens sorrow and sadness amongst the sons of men; and yet I too would be a helper like thee, for are we not children of one home?"

"Thou mistakest things, my brother. Thou dost not see clearly, for I perceive that the 'tears of the immortals' dim thine eyes. When thou touchest men they fall into a longer sleep; but will they, not at the great awakening of all men, hail thee as their friend also? Shall they not come out into a new life blessing thee that thou

hast delivered them from pain and sorrow
and brought them through the death-sleep
out into a joyful and perfect life?"

A light, like the day-dawn shone on
the face of the Spirit of Death as he
embraced his brother, and they twain
soared silently away over the peaks of the
solemn snow-clad hills.

The Spirit of Death as he past, looked
tenderly on the shrunken form of Antonio,
whilst the tip of his wing softly traversed
the colourless brow of the prostrate monk.
There was a quiver of the poor, weary
frame; a sigh trembled on the lips, the eyes
opened with one bright, happy glance, and
he fell into the long sleep which is but the
pathway to the gate of life. The Angel
of Death had touched him.

When his body was discovered by the
monks, the hound was stretched across his
master's knees, dead.

The brothers moved both carefully,
carrying the body of Brother Antonio
tenderly into the little chapel, where he

had spent so many prayerful and repentant hours.

Under his rough garments they found a scrap of vellum fastened by a thread of gold around his neck, and inscribed on it were these names,

Alice,

Anna,

Jean de Longobard.

IV.

THE REFUGEES

IV.

THE REFUGEES.

CHAPTER I.

FATHER AND DAUGHTER.

On a wild spring afternoon two travellers alighted from a sleigh just below the first falls of the Reuss, on the road from the Hospice to Hospenthal; and after liberally paying the driver they bade him return to Airolo as speedily as possible, whilst they themselves proceeded to the village on foot Already the shadows of the coming night-fall were falling upon the landscape, adding to the awful desolateness of the scene, whilst the Reuss as it rushed and roared through the tunnels of snow or dashed over the falls gave intensity to the wildness and loneliness.

The travellers were an old man and a
young girl. The man was tall and dignified,
with long white hair falling to his shoulders,
and walking with difficulty on account of
the feebleness of age. He had the air of
a man who had suffered much and who
still bore patiently the things which were
hard and trying. His companion was a young
girl of about twenty, with the rich brown
skin and dark lustrous eyes of her Italian
race, and every movement and word marked them as belonging to the patrician ranks.
She watched the old man closely and wistfully, regarding him with eyes that shone
with a tenderness which was pitiful in its
soft light of unshed tears; but the old man
went on his way with tottering steps, heed-
less of the pitiful anxiety which followed
him, as his shadow, in the presence of his
only child.

"Father, do you think it was prudent to
dismiss the sleigh so soon?"

"Child, it was necessary. Why do you
ask such a question?"

"I was thinking of you; wondering whether you could bear the long, rough walk into the village below."

"*Bear it?*" And the old man laughed a hard, indifferent laugh. "What have I not borne? These limbs of mine have been weakened by the devilish cruelties of men and by years of solitary confinement in their damp and loathsome dungeons, and now I am again a fugitive fleeing from their hatred and power. They have not crushed the spirit of De la Torre yet, and it is a small thing to bear the walk into yonder village."

A gentle hand was laid on his arm, and a gentle voice said, "Father, I know it all; yes, I know it, but for my sake still be careful."

The old man stopped in his walk, and turning round, said in a voice from which all the fierceness had gone, "Yes, thou knowest it, my child; thou art my only earthly joy and thou wouldest shield me from every harm, for thy love enfolds me like a garment. Yes, I will heed thee and be careful."

For a few minutes they resumed their walk in silence.

"I think, Francesca, I see the village below there, but my eyes are dimmed with suffering and years; is it so?"

"Yes, Father, I can see faintly a group of chalets far below, and to the left a tall tower standing apart."

"Ah! Thou canst see it. That is the Longobard Tower, and we are near to the village of Hospenthal. It is necessary that we should enter it stealthily and under the cover of nightfall so that if possible we may not be seen by anybody."

"Do you think, Father, that we shall find any place of refuge in this village?"

"Yes, for a few days, I think we shall. Jean de Longobard is not of our faith, but he is no unreasoning bigot, and he will give us sanctuary for the sake of old service done to his father and family; and the Longobards had always a secret sympathy with the cause I espouse, and this will at any rate, open their doors to us."

The Longobard Tower, Hospenthal.

"Then you think we shall be safe there, dear Father?"

"Not for long, my child. Those who hate me will stop at nothing if they can get me within their clutches again. They will soon know of our flight and learn its direction and send their minions after us. The Count de la Torre is too prominent a man to be allowed to escape too easily. We shall not be safe until we have crossed the frontier and find our friends in Germany."

"But shall you know the house in Hospenthal and the way to reach it, Father?"

"Yes, I think so. It is many years since I saw it; but long before thou wert born, child, I came here and was able to render a great service to Jean de Longobard's father, which he never forgot. And I remember I was so much impressed by the wild beauty of the position that I think I should easily recognise it again."

Notwithstanding the Count's professed indifference to fatigue it was clear that the difficulties of the descent were telling upon him, and he leant heavily on his daughter's arm, whilst his steps became more feeble and tottering. At length they reached the village, and under the cover of night, without uttering a word, and moving as noiselessly as they could, they found their way unseen to the covered steps which led to the door of the old home of the Longobards.

CHAPTER II.

A REFUGE.

THE Count knocked at the door several times before there was any response to his summons; at length when his patience was well-nigh exhausted, shuffling footsteps were heard coming towards the door, a little shutter was slipped aside, and an old, almost wizened face peered through a little iron grating in the door, and a feeble voice demanded who was there and what was wanted.

"I am Count de la Torre, and I and my daughter ask hospitality from my old friend, Jean de Longobard."

"Signor, I am a feeble woman, old and alone in the house, and I cannot open the door to you to-night."

"Are you not Anna, the old nurse of the Longobards? It seems to me like the voice I heard years ago in this house."

The old woman started like a frightened animal as she heard her name thus spoken.

"Yes, I am Anna."

"For God's sake, Anna, open the door to us, for we are in peril, and I beg for shelter and refuge from those who seek my life!"

At once the great key turned in the cumbrous lock and the door was thrown wide open, as Anna stood aside, holding the ancient lamp in her hand.

"Enter, enter, Signor. I dare not refuse you admission, for my Master's last charge when he left me here years ago, was that I was to give shelter and refuge to any poor hunted creature who should seek them." And after seeing carefully to the refastening of the door she led the way to the sitting-room. Then she carefully covered the windows with their thick, rough curtains, and proceeded to spread the table with such viands as she had in the house. During the meal, which the travellers enjoyed in their hunger, poor and rough as it was, the Count succeeded in bringing back to Anna's memory the occasion of his former visit, and the old servant became more at ease as she began to realise it; whilst her heart warmed towards the sad, weary girl who regarded her steadfastly with her pleading, pitiful eyes.

"And is Jean de Longobard dead?" asked the Count.

"Alas, Signor, I know not." And she told him in a few words the history of his departure. Since then she had heard nothing of him. She had never known of his nearness to her at the Hospice, nor of his death in the great snow-storm. He had, however, carefully arranged for her secure possession of the house as long as she lived, though she knew nothing of this thoughtful care.

"Can you give us any sleeping accommodation?" asked the Count; "for we are weary and exhausted with our journey over the Pass."

"Yes, I can do so in these rooms to-night;

but if you are pursued by foes you would not be safe here longer than the morning. You must go to the Tower by the secret way which is known only to me."

In a short time the Count and his daughter were sleeping the sleep of utter exhaustion,— the dreamless sleep of wor-nout nature; but Anna was keeping vigil again in the old oak chair. The coming of these exiles had stirred many memories, and she could not sleep; and so she sat for hours, talking to herself and living over again portions of her long past life. "The Count and his daughter seem to be kind and good; why should they be pursued by foes, I wonder? —Stop; I remember years ago he made himself bitter enemies among the Church dignitaries and amongst the rulers of the land. He is a political exile once more in his life, and obliged to flee from Italy. And I remember too that he was not of our faith in olden days, and had to be cautious. Yes; I can understand it now, he is hated by the political authorities and detested as a heretic also. But there, that's nothing to me. I hate these persecutions; why can't men let each other think as they like? However, he'll be safe here. He asked 'shelter and refuge,' and I'll see that he gets them. I shall have to fit the Tower up a bit comfortably for him the first thing in the morning."

As soon as the early breakfast was over, Anna took them by a narrow stair down to a dark cave underneath the back of the house. The cave was lined with huge stones built up into a wall with coarse cement, through which there appeared no outlet, and which presented only the appearance of an ordinary cellar used for household purposes. She went to a certain spot and pressed a little knob sunk in the wall, and as she did so one of the big stones which looked as though it were solidly fixed in the wall, began slowly to revolve on its centre until it revealed an opening large enough to creep through without difficulty, and on touching another spring

6

it continued its revolution until the opening was closed. The same means for opening and closing existed on the other side.

"This is the secret entrance to the Tower, and I must ask you to follow me for it is only there you will be safe." And leading the way with a lamp, she conducted them to the sombre apartments of the old Longobard Tower. The Count found the passage rather difficult, but with care and an occasional halt he succeeded in travers- ing it. It was clear that Anna had been busy there from a very early hour, for many things had been done to promote the comfort of the exiles.

"But is not the Tower a very prominent object and likely to be early searched?" asked the Count.

"By no means," said Anna as she smiled. "Men do not know the whereabouts of the secret passage, and there is no other entrance to it except from a great height in the wall, so that no one would think of look- ing for the pursued there. Besides," she added, "it has a terrible reputation for being haunted, and you could not get a soul in the valley to enter it under any circumstances, as it is supposed to be a favourite resort of the devil since he built the Bridge below Andermatt."

The Count smiled contentedly, whilst his daughter pressed Anna's hand and thanked her warmly.

Two days after, whilst Anna was speaking to Francesca, who had come down for some trifling thing for her father, she heard the sounds of strange voices in the road, and then the clatter of arms and foot-steps on the stone stairway.

"Run!" said Anna. "The soldiers are here! You know how to touch the secret springs. I will wait till I hear the stone close before I open the door."

Already the soldiers were pounding on the door and in their impatience were threatening to burst it open, when Anna, assuming as feeble and shuffling a gait as she could, and purposely knocking down a bench with a great clatter, went to the door and peered through the grating, saying in a querulous voice, "What is it, Sirs? Cannot an old woman dwell in peace and quietness without being frightened out of her wits by other folks trying to break into her house?"

"Hold your peace, woman, and open the door," cried the Captain of the band.

"How many of you are there? I should like to know. Because the house won't hold a whole regiment at once."

"Stop talking and open the door sharply, or I will give orders to have it smashed in upon you, you wrinkled old witch."

"Well, I must say that politeness and you seem to have said 'Adieu' to each other, for you don't appear to have much of it left."

"Are you going to open the door, woman?"

"I should like to know who you are first."

"We are officers of justice searching for traitors, you aggravating old hag."

"Why didn't you say so before? Then I should have opened the door quickly, because I should not like to hinder you in so important a Christian affair."

There was a curious sarcastic tone in her voice which made the Captain turn and look at her with a questioning and doubtful air; but she looked him steadfastly and calmly in the face with her keen, black eyes, as though there was nothing unusual in her manner or tone.

"We must search the house all over, and you must accompany us."

"Decidedly. It must be such an awful thing to have the responsibility of searching for heretics and traitors that I shall be pleased to show you every place in the house."

Again there was the strange tone of veiled sarcasm which irritated the Captain, but Anna's manner was as imperturbable as ever.

The closest inspection revealed no sign of the presence of another besides Anna in the house, and the soldiers departed, but not before she had gathered sufficient from their talk to be assured there would be no search of the Tower, because they believed it to be inaccessible to those who had no appliances to scale the walls as far as the opening high up on the southern side.

Later in the day all this was recounted to the refugees in the Tower, and it was deemed desirable to keep entirely within its walls for the next two or three days; and Anna would inform them when it was safe to visit the house again.

CHAPTER III.

THE ESCAPE.

For a day or two the Count seemed entirely prostrate, and could only rest quietly in the rough little bed which had been improvised for him; but on the third morning he appeared to have shaken off all fatigue and weakness, and declared himself ready for further exertions.

"We must not attempt to move yet, Father. Anna says the soldiers are still hanging about the village and it would not be safe."

The old man started up as though impelled by a passion he could not stay.

"Why should this accursed persecution be? Great God, what have we and our fathers done that they and their children should be hounded to death and destruction like this? We who have been only patriots patiently striving to throw off the yoke of oppression and to give the fullest freedom to our down-trodden people, are harassed to death because we have preferred the joys of liberty to the miseries of despotism and tyranny. And some of us are hated all the more because we add the stigma of Protestantism to our love of political freedom; because we make conscience and Christ our chief Masters." And he raised his hand as in entreaty, crying, "How long, O Lord? How long before thou avengest Thy people?"

Francesca laid her gentle hand upon his, but he took no notice.

"It is cruelty,—the cruelty of hell. Long generations ago our family was made to feel the full force of religious and civil persecution, and we have found in modern days that the spirit is not dead. Our persecutors have made our valleys the bitterest Golgothas and our hills the bloodiest of Calvarys, and yet they are called Christians. Oh! it is all a horrible travesty of His teaching, who was just the Incarnation of Divine Love."

"Father, dear Father," pleaded Francesca, "strive to be calm, it will only harm you to act thus."

He stood still and gazed fondly into her eyes. "I will try, Francesca. For myself I care little what happens, but for thee, my child, I care greatly. Thou art my own pet lamb, and I must guard thee still; for thy brothers lie in the unknown graves of the battlefields of national liberty and cannot protect thee; and so thou hast only thy aged father." And he bent his head until it touched hers and his long white hair mingled with the raven-black tresses of his only child.

"I am content. I need no other, if only he be spared and well."

"Ah, thou art too easily contented, Francesca, where thy love is the guide. However, we will do our best to reach our friends in the Rhineland; but it is a long and difficult journey yet."

"Yes, but God will shield and guide us, Father."

"Thou art right, child. I believe He will; and 'what time I am afraid, in the Lord will I hope in His word'."

They were interrupted by Anna's entrance into the Tower, looking excited and alarmed.

"I have bad news to tell, Signor."

"Ah! what may that be?"

"The soldiers are coming to search the house again to-day, and to stop in it for a week."

"How have you learnt that?"

"I overheard one soldier tell another in the village, an hour ago."

The Count looked grave and anxious for a few moments, then said, "In that case we must get away to-night."

"But how, Father, will it be possible for us to leave the Tower?" asked Francesca.

"There is only one way, Signora," said Anna, "and that is by the opening in the wall on the floor above."

"But how can we do that? It opens only on to a deep and awful precipice."

"I must help to let you down by the

rope-ladder which is hidden in the upper story under the floor," said Anna. "It must be done towards midnight, and I will arrange with a nephew I can trust both for his experience and secrecy, to take you in his sleigh. But I must go and make a few needful preparations for your flight. I will return as soon as the soldiers are settled down for the night."

When Anna was gone Francesca crossed over to where the Count was sitting on an oak bench and leaning his elbow on the rough table, as though bewildered and per-plexed; and placing her hand on his shoulder, said, "Father, do not worry about this fresh difficulty. I can bear or do anything to help you; and this sudden departure will only take us sooner to our friends in safety."

He took her hand and kissed it with a courtly reverence.

About an hour before midnight Anna reappeared bearing a few things which would promote the comfort of the fugitives in their cold night journey, explaining to them her inability to come earlier owing to the lateness of the hour at which the soldiers retired to rest.

In a few minutes Anna had drawn out the stout rope-ladder from its hiding-place and affixed it to the strong iron staples which were secured to the wall for the purpose, just as she had been taught to do it by Jean de Longobard on the day he quitted his home. In the dim starlight it seemed but a fragile thing as it hung down the face of the rock, and Francesca shuddered as she looked at it, but Anna assured her it was secure enough, for she knew strong men who had escaped by it even during her remembrance of the Tower.

"Go softly down through the village," she said; "the snow will deaden the sound of your footsteps, and do not speak lest the sound of your voices should arouse the dogs; then go on till you come to the first shrine on the road to Andermatt, where you will find my nephew Paul with

his horse and sleigh. Wrap yourselves up
in the rugs he will bring, and he will drive
you by quick stages to Lucerne, whence
you will find no difficulty in reaching your
friends. Now you must go, you must not
lose more time, or it will be too late to
attempt it."

The Count and his daughter took leave
of Anna with tears, for they understood
how much they owed to her care and
Christian charity.

The Count swung himself on to the
ladder first, and as Francesca saw it sway
to and fro with his weight she had great
difficulty in restraining a wild scream of
affright; but it soon passed as she saw in
the partial obscurity that he landed safely
on the ground. She then embraced Anna
tenderly, and with a smile, swung herself
on to the swaying ladder without hesitation,
for now that her father was safe, she had
no fear for herself, and in a few moments was
standing by his side.

Anna watched their dusky forms turn

down the village street, and then hauling
up the ladder, she stowed it away carefully in its hiding-place, and removing all
traces of recent habitation from the Tower,
went to her room to try to rest and to
avoid arousing suspicion.

The Count and Francesca went softly
and silently down the road until they came
to the rough figure of the Crucified standing by the wayside, where they found
Anna's nephew waiting with the sleigh for
them, and in a few minutes they were
passing quickly through Andermatt on their
way to Flüelen.

When a week had passed away, Anna
heard from Paul that the fugitives had
made good their escape into the realms
of civil and religious freedom, and had found
rest and safety amongst well-known and
long-tried friends, who had welcomed them
with the warmest cordiality and utmost
satisfaction.

By that time the soldiers had quitted
Hospenthal, foiled and disappointed, and

not without a strong suspicion that in some unaccountable way Anna had been the cause of their failure. She herself stood in her old place at the top of the stone steps when they left, and waved a polite but sarcastic "Adieu" to the Captain; then went in, and sitting down in her master's old chair, laughed softly to herself in her quiet content, feeling that she had done just what Jean de Longobard would have had her do in these circumstances. Then as she heard the Vesper bell she threw a dark shawl round her shoulders, and stealing quietly into the church, she offered her service of gratitude and praise to God.

V.

AN URSEREN SINGER

V.

AN URSEREN SINGER.

CHAPTER I.

THE SINGING-BOY.

HE was only a cow-boy, but the gift of
song was in him. Louis was the only child
of the widow Bourget. She was as poor as
she could well be, and found it a difficult
thing to live even in the one-roomed chalet,
which stood close under the mountain above
the Gorge at Hospenthal. It was a lonely
spot, and very difficult of access during the
long, dreary months of winter, but then it
was small and cost but little. As soon as
he was able, Louis was sent out as a herd-
boy to look after the cows which grazed
on the higher slopes during the summer,
and found the days long and wearisome,

spent in this monotonous round of keeping
ward over the wandering herds.

When quite a little lad he had been
trained for the church choir, and the sweetness and purity of his voice had made the
people marvel, and when it was known that
he would sing a solo the church would be
crowded with the villagers, for they were
wont to say it was "like one of the angels
of God singing to men" when the lad's
clear voice rang through the church, and
then went wandering in its sweetness out
at the open door towards the old Tower.
Not seldom the tourists who were passing
through Hospenthal would stop and spend
the Sunday in order to hear the "Boy
Singer" in the church.

He was always singing; song seemed to
ripple from his lips like water from a foun-
tain, and travellers as they passed over the
St. Gothard were often arrested in their
journey by hearing the silvery notes of
melody drop apparently from some snow-
covered peak, as though a white-clad angel

were standing there, and singing down to
the dark valleys of human sin and suffering
a message of the Christ-love from the
harmonies of Heaven. Many of them would
cross themselves and go on their way full
of wonder, all unconscious of the singing
lad amongst the herds.

Louis knew it not, but his melodies were
"song ministries" to the people about him.
Many a toiling, care-worn peasant woman
as she trudged with weary feet under the
weight of a heavy burden, stopped to listen,
and then went on her way with lighter step
because some soft air had put cheering into
her spirit. Many a struggling man had caught
a gentle inspiration as he listened on the
hill-sides, and bore himself more bravely
and patiently in the struggles of his hard
battle of life. And as the sweet music floated
about them, many a soul, stricken down by
the beating storms of sickness or death,
caught a sound of a helping voice speaking
in the dark clouds of doubt or sorrow, of
a Divine Light and Helper, as men heard it

long ago on the slopes of Hermon. But of
all this the singer knew nothing; and so
men and women everywhere, who go on
their way doing their work in untiring
patience and sweetness of heart, are made
divine ministrants of help and blessing to
their fellows without any consciousness of
it in their own spirits. Like the Master they
"please not themselves," so like Him also
they leave behind them a track of cheering
and comfort wherever they go.

Bye-and-bye, however, there came a
change to Louis. As usual one Sunday
morning, he rose in the choir to commence
a solo, when instead of his familiar, clear
notes, there was a painful huskiness in his
voice, and then a high note seemed to strain
and crack. This was repeated, and at the
close his voice seemed to be only a hoarse
croak. His voice had broken, but he did
not understand; and he sank down in his
seat and buried his face in his hands,
whilst his sobs were audible all over the
church. Then with a wild impulse, he rushed

into the sacristy, and tearing off surplice and cassock, he opened the door and ran wildly home.

"Mother!" he cried, as he rushed in; "I can't sing any more."

"Not sing any more, Louis? What do you mean?"

"My voice is gone."

"Your *voice* gone, my lad? Why, you must be dreaming; or else you have got an attack of fever."

"No, no, Mother. Nothing of that sort. My voice turned to a croak like a crow's in the anthem, and I ran out of church."

"What, before the benediction? Oh dear! Louis, whatever will Monsieur le Curé say about such conduct?"

"I can't help it; I shall never sing again." And he fell prone on the floor and sobbed as though his heart would break.

When the tempest of feeling had ceased he lay like one dead for some time, heeding neither his mother's touch nor words; then suddenly starting up, he shuddered, and ran swiftly out of the house and up towards a lonely hollow on a lofty neighbouring height. Here he stood up, and putting his shoulders back, he began the same air he had tried to sing in the church. The result was the same; his voice was broken. As he realised it fully he threw himself prostrate on the rocks and quietly wept himself to sleep. When he awoke the stars were peeping out faintly in the sky, and he felt cold and hungry, and at once he went sadly down to the lonely and quiet chalet.

For a long time Louis never tried to sound a note; his discomfiture had been so complete that no efforts of others could induce him to try. The travellers heard no longer the "angel melodies" on the hills, and the weary men and women went to and fro without the cheering which had heretofore brightened their lives.

Nearly three years later, on a bright June morning, Louis felt an unaccountable impulse within him to sing; he resisted it and strove

resolutely to overcome it, but in vain, he
felt he *must* sing. As soon as he could
he climbed up to the same spot where he
proved his failure of voice before. He
stood with a resolute spirit and began a
well-known air. Yes! he could sing. His
voice rang out sweet and resonant. His
eyes shone, and his frame trembled with
excitement as he essayed the well-remem-
bered solo of his failure. It was perfect.
It was not the same voice, but it was more
beautiful in its roundness and scope. His
voice had become a clear, sweet tenor.
As he continued his efforts his excitement
grew keener, and he sat down and wept
for very gladness. He resolved to tell
no person until he had proved his power;
and so each day he climbed to his
lonely eyrie and exercised his voice
thoroughly. Travellers and others began
to hear again snatches of sweet airs and
songs, and they said, "Surely another angel-
singer has been sent to sing sweet songs
to men"; for the tones dropped like

liquid notes from the heights into the valleys below.

A year or so later, Louis was shown early one morning into the Curé's study. He was now a fine, well-grown young man, bidding fair to be a handsome fellow. He told the story of the last few years to the Curé, and begged to be allowed to sing a well-known solo in the service the next Sunday morning. After some demur and a short trial of his voice the Curé consented, promising to make all necessary arrangements for him, and to keep it secret.

The Sunday morning broke in a glow of summer splendour, the Urseren valley shimmered with the changing lights on rock, and snow, and verdure, and seemed filled with a calm fallen from the eternal quiet of the eternal hills. The church was crowded with villagers and visitors. Louis had taken his place in the choir, amidst the muttered wondering of the singers, who could not understand his presence there, and had no opportunity to ask for explanations. At length, in the proper place, the organist touched a few chords, and a strange voice began a well-known tenor air. At first the voice was tremulous and low, but soon it grew firm and full, and filled every corner of the building with its sweetness. Its tones rose and fell in richest cadence, and seemed to throb with the pulsations of a quickened soul. The sturdy peasants drew themselves up and wondered whence came the melody,—for the singer stood unseen except by a few,—and weary women sobbed as they knelt and clasped their hands in prayer; and when the air ceased and the last notes died away, there was a pause and then a sigh of relief as the pent-up feeling relaxed.

As soon as the service was over there was a general enquiry after the singer, but he could not be found, for Louis had slipped out quietly and quickly by the nearest door; but this time with the joy of a new-born power in his soul, instead of the crushing grief of a hopeless failure.

Sitting near the west door had been a kindly-looking stranger who had evinced the strongest interest and astonishment in the efforts of the singer, and who, at the close of the service sought an interview with the Curé to gain some information concerning him.

CHAPTER II.

THE next day Louis was busy with his usual work when he heard a stranger asking for him by name. He came forwards from the shed in which he was occupied, and found himself confronting a tall, well-dressed, middle-aged Italian.

"You do not know me; my name is Viardot, and my home is at Milan. I was in the church at Hospenthal yesterday, and heard you sing."

Louis looked up with a smile, as he stroked his budding moustache.

"Your name is Louis Bourget, is it not?"

"Yes, Signor, it is."

"You are fond of music?"

"Ah, yes, Signor; indeed I am."

"You have a good voice, but it needs much training and culture."

"Alas, Signor, I know it; but I know too I can never have them."

"Why not?" asked the stranger, although he knew well he had no means.

Louis laughed a cheery, good-tempered laugh, as he replied, "That is easy to see. I am the only child of a poor widow, and I have no money to spend on such things."

"You would like it, I suppose."

Hardly any need for a reply in words; the flashing light in the eyes, the tremulous movement about the lips, and the expression of intenseness on the face were answer enough; but he said earnestly, "I should like it as I love my life."

"Then I think I can help you, my son. I am a Professor of singing at Milan, and if you will come to me I will undertake your musical training. I will pay all costs, and then if you become a successful singer you can refund them to me, or if I am dead you can do the same service for some poor fellow who longs to be a singer, but like yourself, has no means to secure the needful training."

Louis looked up with burning cheeks and eager glance, as though he doubted whether he had understood aright.

" Yes," said Signor Viardot, as he smiled benignly into the excited face; "yes, I mean it. Will you accept my conditions?"

"Signor, my heart is too full to thank you as I wish, but I will do my best to be all you desire."

" Good. Come to this address in Milan sometime during the first week in September next, and ask for me." And he put a a card into his hand.

Louis took the hand as it held the card out to him, and kissed it fervently.

" Adieu, my son. Do not forget."

Louis smiled at the idea of forgetfulness in such a case, and watching his friend until a bend of the road hid him from his view, he then ran to the little chalet, which had been enlarged and made more comfortable by Louis' own labour, and seizing his mother round the neck, he kissed her again and again, and then danced her round the room until he reached a chair in which he seated her, and suddenly burst into a peal of happy laughter. The poor woman was overcome with astonishment, and could only look at him with a dazed, anxious expression. She thought he must be losing his senses.

"Louis, Louis, what is the matter?"

"Nothing, Mother.—Yes, everything."

She looked more astonished than ever. Then Louis stood quietly by her and told her the whole story.

At first she could hardly comprehend what it meant; but gradually the meaning and issues grew clear to her mind, and being a woman of strong common sense, she looked them in the face and made up her mind what must be done.

"Louis, my lad, you must go. I see what it means to you. It will be hard to me, but I can bear it if it is for your good. And some day, perhaps, I shall hear of you as a great singer in far-off cities; but you won't forget the Urseren valley and its old faces and friends?"

"Never, Mother. And if ever I am thought a good enough singer to sing in a great public performance, you shall be there to see and hear."

The widow only shook her head and smiled.

In the evening Louis went into the village and sauntered about for hours, hoping to get a glimpse of his benefactor, but he was disappointed, for he learnt that the Signor had quitted Hospenthal early in the afternoon.

When September came, Louis made his way to Milan over the St. Gothard Pass, and was soon settled down to his work under the care of Signor Viardot; and putting his heart into it he made little difficulty of the long, wearisome hours spent in learning and practising; and his master was delighted with his diligence and progress. With the coming of the summer he returned to Hospenthal, but promised the Signor that he would not be induced to sing to any auditors during his absence. He had great difficulty in doing this, for his old friends put his silence down to every reason but the right one, and began to look on him as growing proud. The Curé understood it and put him right with the villagers; but advised him not to come again until he could sing in the church.

When two years had passed the master began to make plans and arrangements for his appearance in a grand concert, feeling sure he would make his mark and become "a star" in the musical world. At length the long-looked-for night arrived, and full of the spirit of song, cultured by the highest art, he stood before the great crowd, calmly waiting to speak to them in the truest voice of his being. His lips parted, and the golden notes fell on the electrified audience in such marvellous sweetness and power that they could not wait for the conclusion of the song before they filled the hall with their loudest "bravas" and applause. He accepted it all with the utmost calmness and dignity; but he had no eyes for anybody in that splendid crowd except for a sun-burnt woman in a Swiss peasant's dress, who sat immediately in front of him, and looked up with her tear-dimmed eyes full of love and wonder, into the handsome singer's face, whilst her rough and toil-stained hands were folded in a sweet and blessed content. When the concert was over the singer went straight to where she sat, and smiling happily, he offered her his arm and led her out before the wondering and admiring host.

In a few months his fame was in all the great cities of Europe, and his voice was the delight of all.

When next he came to Hospenthal his first business was to settle his mother in a comfortable house, and to sing in the village church; and then, most astonishing of all to the village folk, to make the timid, gentle, little Rose Seiler—the carpenter's only child—his happy wife. His unspoken love had been hers from boyhood and she seemed somehow to understand it, but she little thought she would become the wife of one of the greatest singers in the world, and one of the truest and best of men.

VI.

THE CHILD OF THE AVALANCHE

VI.

THE CHILD OF THE AVALANCHE.

CHAPTER I.

ZUMGOLPH.

MATTIE Mégros had been known as the "Child of the Avalanche" nearly all her life. She is a middle-aged woman now, busy with life's cares and anxieties, but she is always ready to stop and tell you the wonderful history of her childhood.

About half way between Hospenthal and Realp, there is, standing on the rising ground to the left as you go towards the latter village, a little chapel of the simplest and homeliest character. By the side of it stand two houses, the one a small, strongly built cottage, which is the residence of the Curé, and the other a large and ordinary Swiss dwelling, which bears various signs of having passed through some special stormy ordeal.

These dwellings are all that remain to-day of the once large and thriving village of Zumgolph.

For a considerable distance towards the base of the mountains the ground is outlined with the stone foundations of houses, which give a clear idea of the space once covered by the village, and it is not inaptly described as a Pompeii above ground. Close behind it and far above it stands part of the immense St. Gothard group. Overlooking the village there is a deep indentation in the mountains, a valley high up between two peaks. For years this spot had been filling with the débris scattered by storms, and huge masses of snow, until at last the piled up mass broke away and fell as one of the most terrible avalanches the district has ever known. With an awful bound it came down on the doomed village, casting in a few minutes the houses of the peasants to the ground, leaving hardly one stone upon another in some places, and then, sweeping across the road, it mounted for some distance the slopes on the other side of the valley, destroying everything which came in its course.

The chief sufferers were the women and children, who were nearly all destroyed, the men escaping because they were all engaged in the construction of the new carriage road over the St. Gothard. The news soon spread, and reaching the men, they left their work and trooped hurriedly towards Zumgolph, only to find in many a case their homes swept away, and mothers, wives and children lying dead under the rocks and rubbish which the avalanche had brought down, or buried beneath the timbers and stones of the fallen houses. Strong men who feared to face no danger nor peril amongst the hills, sat down and wept like little children. It was to them a real Golgotha and a bitter Gethsemane. In this land of death and valley of desolation no hand has ever attempted to rebuild the village; it remains much as it was immediately after its overthrow more than fifty years ago.

It was about four o'clock on an early Spring afternoon when the avalanche fell, and Mattie's mother who heard the first premonitory sounds, looked up and saw what was coming. She had lived too long in the Alps not to know what horrors it must bring, and giving one despairing cry, she caught up her baby and tossed her through the open window; the child falling under a balcony projecting near. The crash came, and the masses of stone and snow were swept all around her, making the old house shake and totter to its fall, whilst a great beam falling across the room, struck the back of her head and rendered her insensible, and then wedged her helplessly in a corner.

Here and there the moans of some wounded and dying woman were heard, whilst the shrill cry of some little child proclaimed its pain and terror, but very soon an awful death-silence brooded over the scene, and it might have been ages since a populated village had stood under the shadow of the St. Gothard, instead of a few hours.

By the time all the men arrived from the several parts of the new road they were making, the moon had risen and flooded the valley with its light. Amongst the first to arrive was Robert Mégros, the father of Mattie, and with a wild eagerness he began to search amongst the ruins for his young wife and child. As he groped about he heard a moan of pain under the fallen timbers of his old home, and at once redoubled his energy to reach the imprisoned sufferer. In a short time he had cleared the débris away sufficiently to get to the body, and found it was his wife. She was alive, but still insensible; and tenderly draw· ing her from under the beams, he carried her to a grassy plot and laid her gently down. The cold air soon revived her, and after a fit of convulsive sobs she was able to speak.

"Oh, Robert, Robert, take me away, it is so awful," she cried, as she flung her arms round his neck.

He pressed her to his bosom with a strong grip of grateful love.

In a few minutes she started up wildly, crying, "Where is baby? Have you found her, Robert?"

"No. I could see nothing of her. She was not with you under the ruins of the house."

"Not with me, Robert? *Not with me?*" And she clasped her forehead with her hands, as though despairingly searching for something which her memory was unable to recall.

"*Not with me?* Oh, I remember now; when I heard the first rumbling on the mountains I knew what it meant, and I caught her up and threw her through the open window on to the grass, hoping to save her life even if I were crushed myself under the ruins. I must go and find her."

"No, Marie. No. Stop here. I will go."
And placing his wife on the grass, he ran
towards the place where the baby must
have fallen. After peering about for some
minutes, he saw that the balcony of the
next house had fallen in a body, at one
end leaving a space between it and the
wall behind. He crept in here and found,
safely protected by the fallen balcony, the
sleeping form of his little child. Her cries
on being hastily lifted up, soon convinced
him she was unharmed, and covering her
face with kisses, he went and placed her
in Marie's arms. The touch of the baby's
fingers seemed to bring healing and peace
to her as she fondled her tenderly through
her quietly falling tears.

Marie and her child were amongst the
few who were saved from the awful destruction which fell upon Zumgolph; and so
Mattie has always been known as the
"Child of the Avalanche."

For a long period after, no avalanche
fell on this spot, but when fifty-five years

had passed, in the same month, but later in the evening, as the few inhabitants were gathered for their evening prayers, and the valley was shrouded in the nightfall, the same sound of terror was heard again, and the few people who were assembled together stood paralysed with fear and in mortal dread of the expected catastrophe. They heard the terrible *swish* through the air as the avalanche crashed down into the valley, and they felt certain they must be overwhelmed; but, as if by the special interposition of Providence, they were untouched. As soon as they realised their escape they grasped each other's hands and tremblingly sang a hymn of praise.

In the first dawning of the April morning the Curé went out to discover the results and damages. He found that the avalanche in falling had slightly changed its course, winding around the solitary chapel and houses instead of coming against them, hence their marvellous escape.

As soon as he could the Curé walked

over to Hospenthal to tell the tidings to Mattie and her mother, who, though old and feeble, was able to understand what had happened, and trembled as she thus recalled the incident which, fifty-five years before, had named her baby the "Child of the Avalanche."

CHAPTER II.

ON a lovely summer evening a well-built, handsome young Swiss was tramping along the Oberalp road, near to the Hôtel by the Lake. He was the only child of the widowed Madame Faure of Hospenthal, and was studying medicine at Croire. The vacation had begun and he was on his way to the old home.

The Oberalp road passes between some of the wildest ranges of mountain heights, and winds through pastures decked with many varieties of graceful wild flowers, whilst the stillness is broken by the movements of the tawny herds of cattle as they graze, with the tinkling cow-bells fastened round their necks.

As Maurice Faure strode along he suddenly stopped and looked round on this marvellous scene. From the spot where he stood there are splendid views of the wonderful Furka road and heights, the snow-pinnacled group of St. Gothard with its rampart-like walls, and the glittering glaciers of Gurschen and St. Anna. Behind him was the summit of the Calmot whence is obtained one of the most ravishing views amongst the eastern Alps. On either hand the towering hills stretch away for miles on miles until they are finally lost in the wonderful purple haze. Far in the dim distance the houses of Croire, and in a slumbering hollow the almost entirely hidden village of Disentis, like a coy maiden unwilling to be too prominently noticed.

In these regions we are in the very "cradle of the rivers," for only a few miles below the summit of the Oberalp Pass is found the source of the Rhine; over on the west where the snow peaks look like fleecy clouds as they guard the Furka Pass, is the source of the Rhône; and in the

9

south where the lofty Pizzo Centrale looks down on the "eternal lakes" of St. Gothard, is the birth-place of the Ticino and the Reuss.

Maurice Faure had seen this unique and grand panorama many times, but as the sunset light covered it with shimmering beauty, he stood and gazed upon it for some minutes in an ecstasy of delight. Then he drew himself up and went on his way, with swinging tread, towards Andermatt and Hospenthal.

Close by the old bridge at Hospenthal, which crosses the Reuss a few hundred yards before it mingles with the stream from Realp, stands an old house of striking and substantial appearance. It rises in five stories to a sharp, central gable, and its windows are surrounded by some ornament-al designs painted in brown on the stucco front, and relieved by a few touches of vermillion. The whole is faded and faint, but still easily discernible.

The house fronts the bridge and is only some twenty feet from the edge of the precipitous bank of the stream. The door in the centre has an unusual decoration in that district, in the shape of a quaint old iron knocker.

Towards the south there is a stone staircase of about thirteen steps and open to the air and storms. This stairway leads to a square stone landing, from which a door with carved panels gives access to the best rooms of the dwelling, and is indeed the chief entrance to the house. Along this side of the house is a broad, grass-grown yard, bounded by some old stone buildings and the roaring river.

Looking from this open yard to the south, one sees the zig-zags of the path which leads to the St. Gothard Hospice; whilst from the same path one can see all that transpires on the stone landing before the panelled door.

In this house dwelt Madame Faure, the widow of a French physician. She herself belonged to an old Urseren family which had occupied a position of wealth long years before, but was now greatly impoverished and almost extinct. She lived at Hospenthal because the house had been bequeathed to her by a member of her own family, and she found it a very desirable addition to her moderate means.

In this quiet household Mattie Mégros had found a home as companion to Madame Faure.

Mattie was a general favourite; everybody was interested in her as the " Child of the Avalanche." She had grown into a splendid girl, and was acknowledged to be the prettiest maiden in Urseren. No one had hair as golden as hers, nor eyes as blue, and no maiden stepped along with form and foot as lithe as hers. She was the sauciest, merriest maid in the village; and when sometimes her mother rebuked her for her light-heartedness and fun, she only put her arms round her neck and said, " Don't trouble about me, Mother;

I'm all right; but I love fun and mischief, and I'm bound to have as good a time as I can whilst I am young."

Her mother could only shake her head and smile.

Mattie was just the girl to captivate a young man like Maurice Faure; and so it happened. He was a handsome fellow, tall, and well built, with a healthy bronzed face and a long, dark moustache. Honourable and upright in all his dealings, and as earnest and grave of manner as Mattie was bright and frolicsome.

He had admired and loved her for a long time, but had said nothing about it. At length in the twilight of a summer evening they met on the stone landing by the panelled door. She would have passed him and gone down the stairway, but he stopped her.

"Mattie, I want to speak to you."

"I cannot stop, Monsieur Maurice, I am in a hurry."

"Nonsense. You are always in a hurry when I am about."

"Ah, you see, Monsieur, you don't know how many things there are to do, and women are always busy."

"Mattie, you *must* stop this evening, I have something to say to you."

"Well, if Monsieur will not be *very* long I will wait, but I cannot wait long." And stroking down her apron with her right hand, she bent her head and smiled mischievously, as she looked at him from the corners of her eyes. "Of course if Monsieur has any message for Madame I *must* stop and hear it."

"It is nothing for my mother; it is for you."

"Oh, is it?" she said, as innocently as if she had no idea of what he meant.

"Yes, Mattie, it is for you. I want to tell you that I love you, and I want you to be my wife."

All this was as melodious music to her, but she would not let him know it.

"Me? Love *me*, Monsieur? Oh, it is not possible." And she laughed heartily.

"But it is true, Mattie. I mean it."

She knew he did, but she kept her knowledge to herself.

"It cannot be, Monsieur. You would never love the poor 'Child of the Avalanche'."

"But it is so, Mattie, and my one desire is for your love in response."

She still stroked her apron in her shy, innocent fashion, and laughed more mischievously than ever.

"What would Madame say about it? She would not like you to marry me," she said, with a laugh that hardly concealed her earnestness in asking the question.

"I feel sure that my mother would not persistently object to anything that would make me happy."

"I am not so sure about it in this matter."

"Well, I think she would not hinder me; but that is not the question to-night. What I want to know is whether you return my love."

"O dear, I could not possibly tell you now; it would be too difficult, and I really *must* go." And she slipped deftly past him. and ran down the steps.

A pair of keen eyes had watched this scene from the zig-zag path, astonished and angry at what they saw. Madame Faure had been suspicious that something of this kind might happen some day, but she never thought it might be near, and now, as she stood there watching them she felt that something must be done; but what? She would speak to Maurice without delay.

The same evening when the house was quiet and Mattie had gone to bed all un-suspicious of what Madame knew or had seen, she said suddenly to Maurice, "I want to speak to you, my son, about a serious matter."

"All right, ma chére Mére. I am at your service," he said, laying down the paper he was reading.

"As I was coming down the road above the Gorge this evening I saw you talking to Mattie at the top of the steps."

"It was so, Mother."

"It seemed to me you were talking very earnestly, and I should judge by your manner very affectionately."

"That is true also, Mother. I was telling her I loved her, and asked her to be my wife."

"Surely, never. How could you so far forget yourself and your position, Maurice? Such a thing can never be; it would be a disgrace to us."

"Stop, if you please, Mother. I cannot listen to such things. Whether it can ever be depends on Mattie, not on myself. If I can induce her to listen to me, it *must* be. I have told her I wish it, and a Faure is never false to his word."

"Maurice, how can you be so infatuated? Wait, and the fancy will pass away."

"Never, Mother. It is years since I first loved her, but I have never spoken of it till to-day."

"Think, my son, of your position and the unsuitability of such an alliance."

"I have thought of it, until I have been

sickened by it, and determined not to be influenced by any such considerations; and you must not forget, Mother, that a man raises the woman he marries to his own position. Do you know anything prejudicial to Mattie's character or conduct?"

"No, Maurice, no; but the thought of it wounds all my social instincts."

"You have taught me all my life, Mother, to be upright and straightforward, and urged me always to be true to myself if I would be true to others. And if I am to be true to myself now, I must be true to Mattie."

She had never dreamt that this quiet, gentle son of hers had gained such force of character and will; it was a new revelation of the man in him to her wondering eyes. She felt helpless. He had passed, under the power of a pure love, from her old dominion over him, and she knew once for all, that neither anger nor suasion would move him from a course which he deemed to be just and honourable. She sat in

silence for a few moments, then smothering
her own feeling, she rose, and putting her
hand on his shoulder, said with greatest
tenderness, "Maurice, I have only one
thing to ask, wait a year before you do
anything decisively in this matter."

He sat gazing thoughtfully on the floor
for a short time, then looking up and
taking her hand and kissing it fondly, said;
"Mother, I promise. And I trust you not
to treat Mattie with harshness or unkind-
ness in anything."

Madame Faure made no response; but
simply saying " Good night ", she slowly
left the room.

CHAPTER III.

THE next day things reverted to their normal condition at the House by the Bridge, and save that Madame was paler and more dignified than usual there was nothing to indicate that a domestic crisis had happened on the previous night.

The Autumn had come with its early frosts and snows, even earlier than usual in the Urseren valley. Maurice had gone back to Croire, but not before he had had a plain understanding with Mattie, who knowing something of what his mother thought and felt, had grown much more quiet and thoughtful since his departure. Madame said nothing to her that was not kind and considerate, but a feeling of restraint grew up between them; yet it was clear that she considered Mattie in all things, but nothing would induce her to talk about Maurice. This dignified silence grieved the bright, mirth-loving girl sorely, and many a night she cried and sobbed herself to sleep, for she loved Maurice with all the force of her nature.

In the first weeks of November a severe frost set in, and Madame Faure essaying to go down the stone steps, slipped and fell from the top, striking her head against the keen edge of the lowest step. She was stunned by the violence of the fall and lay helpless on the snowy ground. Mattie heard the cry which accompanied the fall, and running out, got her carried to her room.

For many days she lay insensible, and when at last she recovered consciousness she remained too weak to speak or move. Mattie took sole charge of her, and waited on her day and night with the tenderest care, and evidently Madame could not bear to have her out of the room. At length there came a day when Mattie's devoted attention was rewarded, and the invalid was able to sit up.

"Mattie, I can never thank you enough for your loving care and attention, but for them I should have passed away weeks ago."

"Oh, Madame, do not think of it; it has been only a pleasant duty."

The invalid was silent for some moments, then she called Mattie to her and took her hand in one of hers, softly stroking it with the other.

"Mattie, I have been proud and resentful, but it has all gone now. I know your worth, and I have learnt to love you. You must forgive me, and remember I am an old woman who has been brought up in the midst of strong class prejudices."

Mattie knew what all this must mean to Madame, and her eyes filled with tears.

"I am glad," she continued, "that my son will soon be home again. You will be glad too when he comes, Mattie."

The blushing girl only whispered, "Yes,"

but there was a world of happiness in her voice and smile.

Maurice came on Christmas Eve, and on Christmas Morning his mother called both of them to her side, and taking Mattie's hand, she placed it in his, saying, "Maurice, she is worthy of you and of your love. May God bless you both!"

They were married in the Spring: Mattie only asking that the ceremony might take place in the little chapel at Zumgolph and that the dear old Curé should officiate.

Madame Faure lived long enough to see and spoil her first two grandchildren, and then peacefully passed away in the presence of her children, leaving them in possession of the House by the Bridge; and nobody was more loved and honoured in the valley than Doctor Faure and his wife, the " Child of the Avalanche."

VII.

GASPARD.

A view from the summit of the Furka Pass.

VII.

GASPARD.

CHAPTER I.

AN OBERLAND GUIDE.

THE Furka Pass was filled with the soft light of a lovely June evening. It had been a cold, wild spring, and this had been the first really fine day of the early summer-time, and a few tourists had been lured to the Furka by the clear blue sky and brilliant sunshine.

Two Englishmen stood on the green in front of the Furka Hôtel, looking on the Bernese Alps before them. It was their first view, and as they stood leaning on their alpenstocks they spoke not a word, the awe of the mountain glory was upon them as a spell. Whilst life should last they would never forget it. Before them stood the huge pile of the Finsteraarhorn, to the right the pointed summits of the Shreckhorn, the gleam of the distant Silberhorn and the masses of the Monch and Eiger. They were almost covered with snow, only long strips of dark rock, like giant ribs, pierced it here and there. The sun was just going down, and the whole range shimmered in that soft, quivering, silver light, which is only seen on snow mountains when the sun begins to disappear, and then changes to the burning fire of the mountain afterglow.

A deep sigh broke the spell and the silence, and they turned to speak to a guide who stood waiting near.

Gaspard Zähringer was just the type of a young and courteous Swiss guide. His skin browned by exposure to the sun and storm, dark hazel eyes, and white teeth shining when he smiled beneath his long tawny moustache. His swinging step firm and even, suggestive of long tramps and dangerous climbing.

Gaspard was one of the Meiringen guides, but he seemed to seize every possible occasion which gave him a reasonable excuse for coming to the Furka. The weather was never too wild nor too stormy for any expedition which brought him within walking distance of the Furka Hôtel. The thing puzzled his comrades, and he never enlightened them; but the reason was not far to seek to those who could read "the signs of the times." Whilst he stood with his employers on the green his eyes were eagerly scanning the windows of the Hôtel, searching for something he desired to see. Presently, a bronzed, laughing face peeped out of an upper window. Gaspard saw it and doffed his cap, whilst a happy smile spread over his dark countenance. The only answer was a mischievous pursing of the lips and shake of the head, whilst a saucy light twinkled in the dark brown eyes.

Marie Meyer was an orphan girl from Hospenthal, and for two seasons had been chambermaid at the Furka Hôtel; a bright, laughter-loving, saucy maiden, but with a heart as tender and a love as true as a maiden's heart and love can be. Gaspard Zähringer had first met her two years before at a village fête, and had sought again and again to win her promise to become his wife, but Marie was coy and not easy to win. She loved him fondly enough, but took great pains to lead him to suppose he was much the same as all other men to her.

When the moon was shining down on the great snow peaks, and the Hôtel was quiet for the night, Gaspard and Marie met under the rock at the foot of the Furka-horn. Marie was unusually calm and solemn as Gaspard pressed his suit and urged her to make him happy by promising to be his wife.

She only shook her head.

"I do not think it is possible, Gaspard."

"Not possible, Marie, why not?"

She made no reply.

A fierce light of passion flashed from his
eyes, and he set his teeth together in a
paroxysm of determination. He felt he
could not give her up without a mighty
struggle with his own heart.

"Is there another you love better than me,
Marie?"

"You should not ask."

"I must ask. I *must* know. My life
depends on it. Tell me, Marie; is there
anybody between us?"

"No. No, Gaspard," she replied quickly,
for his intense earnestness awoke her fear-
fulness.

The tension of his feeling was lessened,
and the fierceness died out of his eyes.

"You love me, Marie; I know you do."

"How can you know such a thing?"

"I can read it in your eyes."

"Oh, nonsense. That is just the way
with you men."

"Well, it is true now, isn't it?"

She only laughed mischievously at him.

"Marie, don't send me away miserable

this time. You have kept me waiting so
long already for your promise that I feel
I shall soon lose all hope and heart if you
send me away again without it."

She could see his eager eyes shining in
the moonlight, and she felt she must not
trifle longer with his faithful love.

"Marie, will you be my wife when the
early winter snows cover the mountains?"

A sudden solemnity fell on the merry
mountain maiden, and she bowed her head
on her breast.

"Marie, say yes; and I shall be the
happiest guide in the Oberland."

For a few moments she stood silently
looking up towards the white peak of the
Galenstock, then she turned slowly towards
him, and putting her hand in his, said
softly, "Yes, Gaspard; I will."

One long embrace and a fervent "God
bless thee," and these two stood under
the silent, snow-clad hills solemnly betrothed
to each other as man and wife.

CHAPTER II.

A FORTNIGHT later a party of tourists and guides was coming down the snow slopes of one of the highest of the Bernese Alps; they were roped together in the usual way, Gaspard being the leader of the party. The ascent had been very successful, and they were in the highest possible spirits.

In the midst of their laughter and mirth Gaspard suddenly disappeared; a snow bridge had given way as he stepped upon it, and an awful strain was felt on the rope, as though the others would be drawn after him; and at once they threw themselves into the safest position to resist the dragging force of the suspended guide. This was hardly done when, without any warning, the rope snapped like a thread, and with one wild cry Gaspard fell into the

crevasse which the snow bridge had partly
hidden. When the echoes of that one awful
cry had died away, no further sound was
heard, and the solemn silence of the mountains seemed like a burden of woe and awe
on the spirits of the others.

A guide crept to the edge of the precipice, and looking over, saw the body lying
wedged on a ledge of rock near the bottom
of the great fissure. A few minutes thought
and consultation decided them what to do.
At a lonely hut built for mountaineers not
far away they would possibly find other
guides and ropes. One of them started at
once, for daylight was precious. On reaching the hut, he found two guides there who
readily consented to return with him; for
Swiss guides are loyal men and would not
leave a comrade in distress whilst any hope
of help remained.

They looked over into the abyss, and
shuddered as they realised the danger. At
length the youngest of the four, whom they
called Jean, a fine, bright fellow from Zer-

matt, took a second look over the brink;
then he bared his head and looked up to
the deep blue sky.

"The good God will take care of me.
You can lower me over with the rope."

The others could only grasp his hand.

"If anything happens to me, lads, give
a thought to my old mother and don't let
her starve. She has got nobody but me to
help her."

The others raised their hands in solemn
pledge, and cried as with one voice, "We
will."

They secured one well-tested rope around
him and lowered him till his feet rested on
the ledge of rock, then they lowered the
second rope; this he fastened around the
body of Gaspard, with great risk and difficulty, for the ledge was narrow and slip-
pery, and below him on one side yawned
an awful black gorge into which one false
movement might plunge him. When he had
carefully arranged the rope, he took it
firmly in his hand and called to his com-

rades to pull him up. It was a perilous journey and he trembled as he thought of the
fragile cord on which he hung, but he knew
the men above were brave and true and
strong. Yet brave as they were, they were
unspeakably glad when he was safely raised
again to the snow plateau on which they
stood. The next thing was to take the rope
which he held in his hand and raise the
body of Gaspard. This was done with the
greatest gentleness, and difficult as it was
to land the helpless form over the edge of the
precipice, success crowned their patient
efforts and they laid him at full length on
the soft snow. They thought him quite
dead, but as they moved him a quiver of
the frame and a moan of pain shewed them
their mistake and awakened a dawning hope
in their minds. They succeeded in getting
him down to the little hut in spite of fearful obstacles, and here he lay for days
entirely unconscious. In the meantime appliances were sought in the valley; and with
better aids, they got him down to his

widowed sister's chalet near to Meiringen.

The doctors said it was possible that he might live and recover consciousness, but he would never be able to walk again. It was a dark and sorrowful outlook for Gaspard and his friends.

CHAPTER III.

A LOYAL MAIDEN.

It was a strangely wild and windy night for the month of July even amongst the Alps. The mists rolled over the Furka, like great cloud-billows, blotting out mountain and valley and making everything feel as chilly as a damp October night. The doors of the Hôtel were all closed, and the wind battered against them like besieging foes, and then swept away over the St. Gothard, moaning like a great spirit in pain.

The travellers who were there were thankful for the warmth and shelter, only hoping the storm would spend itself during the night so that they might go on their way on the morrow.

Two guides were sitting at a table, talking seriously over their lager beer.

" Are you making any excursion from here, Jean?"

"No, I am going down to Zermatt to-morrow. I feel I should like a little rest after the experiences I've had lately."

"Why, what has happened then?"

For answer he told the story of Gaspard's accident and his own part in the rescue.

During the narration, Marie Meyer had entered the room, and hearing Gaspard's name mentioned, had stood quietly to listen.

The backs of the speakers were towards her, and as she stood in a deep shadow they did not notice her. As the story was unfolded by Jean she grew whiter and whiter—the room swam round—her heart stood still—and she gave one clutch at the nearest object and then fell senseless on the floor.

The startled guides sprang from their seats wondering what had happened, not knowing there could be any connection between their talk and Marie's dead faint.

During the night the storm had spent itself, and the morning broke in glowing sunshine. At daybreak, the hotel door was opened, and Marie stood ready for the long walk to Meiringen; indeed, she had with difficulty been kept from starting in the stormy night. The fresh morning air and the cloudless panorama of the Alps helped to soothe her fevered spirit and breathe calmness to her heart. With the step of a strong mountain maid she sped down the long zig-zags of the Pass, only stopping to gaze a moment on the grand view of the Weisshorn and the Matterhorn which met her view at a bend of the road above the glacier. Without stopping she passed the Gletsch and began the rough ascent to the Grimsel; and when she reached the summit she was startled by the magnificence of the scene. She stood alone in a glorious snow-land. The peaks were covered; the Todden-see was one mass of ice, and here and there her path lay between snow banks twenty feet in height on either hand, cut out at great cost and labour; whilst the old Hospice was snowed up at one end to its second floor. Preoccupied as she was, the scene nevertheless was permanently imprinted on her mind.

In the early evening she reached Meiringen and soon found her way to Gaspard's home. He had recovered consciousness the day before, and as Marie opened the door he turned his face towards her with one long yearning gaze of pitiful love. His great dark eyes were full of the light of a strong soul smitten as unto death. For several moments neither spoke; for hearts smitten thus have little speech.

"Gaspard, I only heard of it last night, and I have come at once to be with you."

"Marie, I am useless in life now, the doctors say I shall never walk again. You must try to forget me and leave me to my misery."

"Gaspard, never say that again. I am your betrothed, and you are dearer to me than ever."

II

"But you must not waste your life and your time on me; I am like a broken forest pine."

"Do not say so. Let me think my own thoughts, Gaspard, and leave me to my own ways."

Through long weeks she nursed and tended him, until he was able to be carried out to sit in the late autumn sunshine.

One day as she sat by his side, whilst he was busy doing some light wood-carving in which he was an expert, she suddenly said, "Gaspard, you asked me to promise to be your wife before the winter snows came, and I promised. When are you going to ask me to fulfil that promise?"

He was so astonished at her question that he dropped his work and turned to look at her in amazement. But she went on with her embroidery and never turned her face towards him.

"Marie, what do you mean?"

"Just what I said;" but still she looked only on her work.

"You cannot be serious."

"But I am." Still she looked only at her embroidery.

"What! Do you mean to say you will have a life-long cripple for a husband? Oh, it cannot be; it would be wickedly selfish on my part to wish you to keep your promise."

"Of course I mean it. If you will not have me for a wife, I shall never have another husband;" and then she turned her eyes upon him, filled with love and tears, whilst a mischievous smile flickered about her lips.

And so they settled it.

The neighbours thought her strangely foolish, but admired her pluck and faithfulness.

A little later a wedding party was gathered in the old village church. The bridegroom was seated in a mountain carrying-chair, but the bride seemed as proud of him as though he were standing in his manhood's strength. When the old Curé blessed them as husband and wife, his voice trembled like a child's, and there was hardly a dry eye in the assembly. The service over, Marie twined her arms about Gaspard's neck and kissed him again and again, whilst he sobbed as a child sobs on its mother's breast when some pain or trouble passes away.

VIII.
THE CRYSTAL SEEKER

VIII.

THE CRYSTAL SEEKER.

CHAPTER I.

WAYSIDE WAITING.

On one of the loveliest of June days two Englishmen were walking down the road from the St. Gothard Hospice towards Airolo. The novelty of the position, the desolate grandeur of the scene, and the crisp mountain air filled their spirits with the wildest exhilaration, and they bounded down the road-way with the utmost vivacity and delight. About a mile or so below the Hospice, in crossing one of the enticing, but treacherous " short cuts " which abound on the Alps, the younger of them fell, and after striking against a large boulder, rolled on to his alpenstock, which had slip-

ped from his grasp and lay across a little
stream of water which came from the melt-
ing snow higher up. The fall crashed the
alpenstock into splinters, and he lay helpless and injured by the roadside.

A message was sent from the Hôtel at
the top of the Pass down to Airolo for
help, and then there was nothing further to
do but to sit waiting by the wayside until
it came. Hardly anything could have been
more solitary and full of awe. The season
had been cold and stormy; only the day
before had the passage through the snow
on the summit of the Pass been made, and
so the whole district was free from travellers and girt in with an awful loneliness.
Hour after hour passed in that weary dragging on which always marks such circumstances, but which served to impress on
the mind, with ineffaceable clearness, the
surroundings of the spot.

Looking upwards to the right as they sat,
was a magnificent view of the wild scenery
around the Lago Grande; the spot looking

like a weird, rock-strewn amphitheatre, without any means of exit save by way of the perilous heights which girdle and guard it all about. Below on the left, the lovely valley stretching away in its deep environment of hills, and its splendid road reaching onwards, like the still coils of a monster serpent, till it is lost in the dim distance of the sweet Italian borderland. Before them the precipitous, rugged Fibbia, rising to nearly nine thousand feet, and along its lower slopes they could see the faint traces of goat-tracks, which looked only like lines drawn across the mountain, on the edges of frightful precipices, and they wondered how the feet of men, even "to the manner born," could retain their footing and tread them safely.

Whilst waiting thus they saw a man rather short of stature rounding the corner of the road above. He bore between his shoulders a strong canvas bag, which served as a knapsack, and carried in his hand an Alpine ice-axe. He was weather-beaten and bronzed, and had the air of a man who had been in the tempests and dangers of the mountains, and he was quickly recognised as a guide. With his coming there came the dawn of help and hopefulness to the watchers. He stood in astonishment for a few moments, and then asked courteously what it meant. A few words in French sufficed to make him understand the position, and at once bringing the experience of his profession to bear, he aided in adding to the comfort and safety of those who waited.

"You are a guide, are you not?" asked the elder of the two.

"Oui, Monsieur."

"Are you returning from some excursion on the mountains near here?"

"Yes, Monsieur. I have been on the Fibbia." And he pointed to the mountain opposite.

"Is the Fibbia dangerous?"

"Well, yes, Monsieur; just now it is so; there is so much snow."

"I suppose you know the Fibbia well."

He smiled as he said, "Yes, *very* well.

"Do you take many tourists up?"

"No, Monsieur; it is not in that way I know the mountain."

"In what way then, do you know it so well?"

"It is because I go there to find crystals."

" *Crystals!* "

"Oui, Monsieur, like these." And he put his hand into one of his capacious pockets and drew out two or three specimens of beautiful rock crystals.

"But you run great risk and danger in getting these crystals, do you not?"

He smiled and shrugged his shoulders.

Thus the hours passed, and the light began to fade from the valley and creep lingeringly up the hills towards the summits, when the sound of wheels was heard, and to the relief of all a carriage it was seen coming up towards the spot where the anxious group sat and watched.

The wayside waiting was over; and in the deepening twilight the Englishmen said

"Adieu" to Jacques Nager, the guide, and were driven down to the village of Hospenthal; the sound of the rushing Reuss never far away, and very distinct in the solemn stillness of the evening hours.

CHAPTER II.

It was not worth calling a "hut"; it was nothing more than a shelter, just large enough to cover Jacques at night or during a storm. He spent so much time on the Fibbia that it became necessary that he should provide himself a shelter of some sort in order to avoid the frequent descents into the valley.

On the south side of the mountain a huge piece of rock jutted out, leaving a hollow open place at its base. A narrow ledge of rock overhanging an enormous precipice led to this spot. To one unacquainted with the Alps it would have seemed altogether inaccessible, whilst to an expert mountaineer it was not devoid of risk and danger. Here, in this hollow, Jacques decided to construct himself a shelter. He first enlarged the space beneath the rock by using his ice-axe to cut away the soil and fragments of stone which partially filled it; these he put carefully on one side for further use. He then carried on his back from the valley, at different times, some strong boards cut to the needed length, which he nailed firmly together until he had made a place sufficiently large to creep into and sit in. Then he piled up the loose stones and débris which he had accumulated, until it was buried beneath them. When this was done he felt he had a safe shelter in which he could sit and pass the night and so be ready to prosecute his search for crystals with the dawn of day.

In the early Spring he had met with the widow of an aged Chamonix guide, who told him she had heard her husband repeatedly say that there were unthought of crystal treasures in some dangerous regions of these mountains, out of the ordinary routes trodden by men; for as a little lad he remembered being lowered with a rope into an awful gorge where no footing could be found and he was quickly drawn up again, but not before he caught sight of the great glistening crystals on the edge of the precipice.

This story fell like fruitful seed into good soil as he listened to it. It enkindled the keenest desires, and awoke the spirit of strongest determination. He brooded over it by day and by night, and his course of action was decided upon as he sat one stormy day in his cramped hut on the Fibbia. The morning had been bright and sunny, but suddenly the sky was overcast and the air became still and oppressive. Jacques knew it portended a heavy storm and he hastened to his hut. From the opening which served as an entrance he had a magnificent view over the valley to the south, and on the west the lonely peaks uplifted themselves in snowy splendour.

Below him a great black cloud seemed hurling itself against the mountain side and emitting, every few seconds, fierce, blazing flashes of light; whilst the thunder pealed like the crashing of an army's artillery amongst the reverberating rocks, and then fell solemnly, like the booming of minute guns in the echoes of the distant peaks. Gradually the storm crept upwards until it enfolded the hut in a burning blaze of light or in a blackness deeper than midnight; whilst the wind roared like the sea in a fury, and the rain fell like an avalanche of water. Through all this wild commotion Jacques sat calmly in his imperfect shelter, which seemed sometimes as though it must be blown over the precipice by the wind, or washed over by the rain. But he sat on, hour after hour, quietly waiting for the storm to abate; yet never troubled by fear nor anxiety about his own safety.

When the night had passed and the morning broke in resplendent glory, as it does break on the Alps after storms, he had made up his mind what to do.

CHAPTER III.

THE St. Gothard group covers a large area, and extends from the Oberalp Pass to the Simplon road in one direction, and from beyond Tessin to the Urseren valley in the other. The St. Gothard is really a lofty, rugged plateau, possessing many lakes, glistening with great glaciers, and seamed with terrible chasms and crevasses; the whole being engirdled by immense mountains. The name was given to it as far back as the twelfth century, by the people of Disentis, who had built a chapel dedicated to St. Gothard, and who thus called the great mountainous group above them by the same name.

The group is rich in certain minerals, and especially in great crystals of felspar, whilst some exceedingly beautiful

12

examples of rock crystal and adular have been found there. Many of these are to be seen in the mineral collections of the neighbourhood and in the museums of the country.

The fact that these specimens are highly prized and therefore of very considerable monetary value, fills the mountaineers with a determination to brave any degree of danger and endure any privations in searching for them.

Jacques was one of the most successful seekers, and his past successes only led him on to run greater risks in the hope of greater gains. He was one of the most indomitable and hardy mountaineers of the Alps, and feared neither storms, snows, nor precipices. He had thought long over the widow's story and the possible presence of crystals amongst the higher peaks, until he had convinced himself that in a particularly lonely and dangerous spot some of. the largest and rarest would be found. At the side of one of the glaciers is a little

mound which in the autumn, after a long
hot summer, shows itself to be covered
with green grass; below this is a great
precipice over which masses of ice fall and
rest on a rocky platform; this overhangs
a deep, black chasm, through which a glacier
stream goes thundering on as it receives
into its dark bosom the falling ice-blocks
and slipping boulders. It was here amongst
these perilous surroundings that Jacques believed he should find extensive mineral
treasures; and contrary to all counsel he
resolved to make the trial. The time of
his intended "tour of discovery" he told
to nobody, wishing to realise for himself
only all the glory and profit to which it
may lead. He determined therefore to go
unaccompanied and unaided. He was so
often away for days and sometimes weeks
together that his absence would cause no
unusual anxiety at home, so he kept silence
as to the dangerous expedition he intended
to make. It was in the month of September,
when the press of the mountaineering season

was beginning to lessen, that he decided
to make his great effort. The weather was
fine and settled, and after making all needful preparations, he started—buoyant with
hope and strong in his expectation of reap-
ing the most substantial advantages.

He was met the next day on one of the
upper slopes by an old companion, and they
spent some time in conversation, sitting on
their knapsacks, on the edge of a still,
dark lake; but he skilfully evaded any
questions as to the purpose or destiny of
his journey.

The next day he was seen by two herd-
boys, who were far below on some slopes
opposite to this perilous place. They saw
a man creeping along the bare face of the
rock and carefully making his way amongst
a mass of ice-blocks which the glacier above
had forced down; and as he crept along
he slipped, and rolling to the edge of the
awful precipice, he fell over and disappeared
into the black chasm below. The boys
were awe-struck and dazed by what they

saw, although it was at so great a distance
from them that their view of it was indis-
tinct. They felt they could do nothing in
the matter, save to mention it to the men
who were with them in the solitary hut
where they passed the night; and these
affected not to believe their story, saying
the distance was too far for them to know
whether it had been a man or no. The
lads shook their heads and held to their
story.

Meanwhile, as the days and weeks flew
by, there was anxiety and fear in the
"Crystal Seeker's" home; and it grew
into a certainty that some calamity had
befallen him, for nothing could be heard
of him in any of his old quarters, and nobody had seen him since the chamois hunter
who had talked with him by the lake.
Vigorous search-parties were organised,
and the most strenuous efforts were used
to discover what had become of him, but
in vain. The only light on the matter which
could be gained was what the herd-boys

could tell to a party of explorers who fell
in with them on the second day of the
search.

"Where did you see it?" asked the old
hunter, who was of the party.

"There," said the lads, as they pointed
to a precipice dim with the distance and
haze.

"What, by that glacier?"

"Yes."

"Oh, mon Dieu! What an awful place
on which to fall! Why, it is just over one
of the most terrible chasms amongst the
mountains."

"Do you think it could be Jacques who
fell?" asked a guide.

"No doubt of it. It was the day after I
met him, and he hinted in a mysterious way
that he might be going in that direction."

"But what should he go there for?"

"Oh, for crystals. There is an old legend
about some magnificent specimens lying
below that naked granite precipice; but
nobody before has been fool-hardy enough

to risk his life to seek those legendary treasures. Poor Jacques was crystal-mad, and thought perhaps the short cut to wealth lay along the edge of that deadly gulf."

"Then he has paid the price, and lost the treasures."

"Just so," responded the hunter, with a distinct tremble in his voice. " Poor Jacques! He was a brave, good fellow."

The search-party did not give up their efforts until they had explored the terrible spot as closely as its perils permitted; the old hunter being securely roped that he might go as near as he could to the edge of the chasm. When he returned he said he could see an ice-axe lying amongst the débris at a distance, which he thought looked like the one Jacques usually carried.

From that day Jacques was always spoken of as "The Lost Guide."

* * *

On a high peak not so far from this spot stands a huge cross, perfectly plain, without figure or inscription upon it. From the valleys and slopes below it is a clear and startling object; and its sharply cut form is outlined on the sky or snow above. On one hand there are the mountains pathetic with the story of a "Lost Guide"; and on the other, they uplift the symbol of a world's salvation. Just in view of the positions where thrilling Alpine catastrophes have occurred, it rears its head in its quiet, majestic symbolism. The mountains speak of power and suffering which may end in *death;* that cross speaks to men of power and suffering which lead to a *life* which is eternal. The great granite peaks of St. Gothard, uprising in their stern and solemn grandeur, shall pass away; but that simple, rough cross speaks of eternal beauty and undying might. The Fibbia and its glory shall perish; but the Calvary and its love shall "endure for ever."

THE END.

NOW BEING PUBLISHED

The New Popular Edition

OF THE

Works of George Meredith

Crown 8vo, 6s. each.

With Frontispieces by BERNARD PARTRIDGE, HARRISON
MILLER, and others.

THE ORDEAL OF RICHARD FEVEREL
EVAN HARRINGTON
SANDRA BELLONI
VITTORIA
RHODA FLEMING
THE ADVENTURES OF HARRY RICHMOND
BEAUCHAMP'S CAREER
THE EGOIST
DIANA OF THE CROSSWAYS
ONE OF OUR CONQUERORS
LORD ORMONT AND HIS AMINTA
THE AMAZING MARRIAGE
THE SHAVING OF SHAGPAT
THE TRAGIC COMEDIANS
SHORT STORIES
SELECTED POEMS

ARCHIBALD CONSTABLE & CO
2 WHITEHALL GARDENS WESTMINSTER

I

In the Tideway

By FLORA ANNIE STEEL

(Author of " Miss Stuart's Legacy," " On the Face of the Waters," etc.)

6s.

" One has grown accustomed to the association of Mrs. Steel's name with novels which deal exclusively with Indians and Anglo-Indians. Such powerful and remarkable books as 'The Potter's Thumb' and 'On the Face of the Waters,' point to a specialism which is becoming one of the salient features of modern fiction; but 'In the Tideway,' although dealing entirely with England and Scotland, presents the same keen and unerring grasp of character, the same faculty of conveying local atmosphere and colour, the same talent for creating strong and dramatic situations, and the same originality of thought and expression. . . . It is too late in the day to speak of Mrs. Steel's position. This is assured, but this book adds greatly to an established position. It is profoundly impressive."—*St. James's Budget.*

"Wonderfully bright and lively both in dialogue and incidents."— *Scotsman.*

"Admirably written."—*Glasgow Herald.*

"The story is beyond question powerful. The characters are life-like and the dialogue is bright and natural."—*Manchester Guardian.*

"As it is, the book is a sheer triumph of skill, one degree perhaps less valuable than a fully conceived presentation of the actual, but none the less admirable within its limits. There is care shown in every character. . . . But the real art, perhaps, lies less in the sequence of events or the portrayal of character, than in just this subtle sugges-tion everywhere of the abiding causeless mystery of land and sea."— *Academy.*

ARCHIBALD CONSTABLE & CO

2 WHITEHALL GARDENS WESTMINSTER

2

Dracula

By BRAM STOKER

" One of the most enthralling and unique romances ever written."
—*The Christian World.*

" The very weirdest of weird tales."—*Punch.*

"Its fascination is so great that it is impossible to lay it aside."—*The Lady.*

"It holds us enthralled."—*The Literary World.*

" The idea is so novel that one gasps, as it were, at its originality.   A romance far above the ordinary production."—*St. Paul's.*

" Much loving and happy human nature, much heroism, much faithfulness, much dauntless hope, so that as one phantasmal ghastliness follows another in horrid swift succession the reader is always accompanied by images of devotion and friendliness."—*Liverpool Daily Post.*

" A most fascinating narrative."—*Dublin Evening Herald.*

" While it will thrill the reader, it will fascinate him too much to put it down till he has finished it."—*Bristol Mercury.*

" It is just one of those books which will inevitably be widely read and talked about."—*Lincoln Mercury.*

" A preternatural story of singular power.   The book is bound to be a success."—*Dublin Freeman's Journal.*

" The characters are limned in a striking manner."—*Manchester Courier.*

" A decidedly able as exceptionally interesting and dramatically told story."—*Sheffield Telegraph.*

" We strongly recommend all readers of a sensitive nature or weak nerves to abstain from following the diabolic adventures of Count Dracula."—*Sheffield Independent.*

"Arrests and holds the attention by virtue of new ideas, treated in an uncommon style.   Throughout the book there is not a dull passage."—*Shrewsbury Chronicle.*

" Singularly entertaining."—*Birmingham Daily Mail.*

" Fascinates the imagination and keeps the reader chained."—*Western Times* (Exeter).

" We commend it to the attention of readers who like their literary fare strong, and at the same time healthy."—*Oban Times.*

" The most original work of fiction in this almost barren season."—*Black and White.*

" We read it with a fascination which was irresistible."—*Birmingham Gazette.*

" The spell of the book, while one is reading it, is simply perfect."—*Woman.*

" The most blood-curdling novel of the paralysed century."—*Gloucester Journal.*

" The sensation of the season."—*Weekly Liverpool Courier.*

ARCHIBALD CONSTABLE & CO

2 WHITEHALL GARDENS WESTMINSTER

3

The Folly of Pen Harrington

By JULIAN STURGIS. 6s.

Green Fire : A Story of the Western Islands

By FIONA MACLEOD,

Author of " The Sin Eater," " Pharais," " The Mountain Lovers," etc.

Crown 8vo, 6s.

The Laughter of Peterkin

A Re-telling of Old Stories of the Celtic Wonderworld.

By FIONA MACLEOD.

Crown 8vo, 6s. Illustrated.

A book for young and old.

Odd Stories

By FRANCES FORBES ROBERTSON.

Crown 8vo, 6s.

The Dark Way of Love

From the French of M. Charles le Goffic.

Translated by E. WINGATE RINDER.

Some Observations of a Foster Parent

By JOHN CHARLES TARVER.

Crown 8vo, 6s.

ARCHIBALD CONSTABLE & CO

2 WHITEHALL GARDENS WESTMINSTER

The Amazing Marriage

By GEORGE MEREDITH

Crown 8vo, 6s.

"To say that Mr. Meredith is at his best in 'The Amazing Marriage' is to say that he has given us a masterpiece."—*Daily News.*

"Mr. Meredith belongs to the great school of writers of whom Aristophanes, Rabelais, Montaigne, Fielding, are some of the most splendid examples. Mr. Meredith's style is not . . . so obscure as it is often represented to be."—*Athenæum.*

"Carinthia will take her place . . . in the long gallery of those Meredithian women whom all literary Europe delights to honour."—*Daily Chronicle.*

"By George Meredith! Those three words have a welcome sound for reviewers."—*Literary World.*

"We have said enough to show that Mr. Meredith's plot is excellently conceived and excellently carried out."—*Standard.*

"Most novels are merely dramas with padded stage directions. Mr. Meredith's, everybody knows, are otherwise. His novels are always human life. . . ."—*The Star.*

"Wholly delightful."—*Black and White.*

"This is a book in which, to use Mr. Meredith's own expression, you jump to his meaning."—*Westminster Gazette.*

"The book is full of wise, deep, and brilliant things."—*Scotsman.*

"This latest example of Mr. Meredith's quality is marked by observation, wit, and variegated fancy enough to deck out a gross of novels of the average sort."—*Morning Post.*

ARCHIBALD CONSTABLE & CO
2 WHITEHALL GARDENS WESTMINSTER

London City Churches

BY

A. E. DANIELL

WITH NUMEROUS ILLUSTRATIONS BY

LEONARD MARTIN

WITH A MAP SHOWING THE POSITION OF EACH CHURCH

Imperial 16*mo*, 6s.

The intention of this book is to present to the public a concise account of each of the churches of the City of London. If any reader should be induced to explore for himself these very interesting, but little known buildings, wherein he cannot fail to find ample to reward him for his pains, the object of the writer will have been attained.

This volume is profusely illustrated from drawings specially made by Mr. Leonard Martin, and from photographs which have been prepared expressly for this work.

"The author of this book knows the City churches one and all, and has studied their monuments and archives with the patient reverence of the true antiquary, and, armed with the pen instead of the chisel, he has done his best to give permanent record to their claims on the nation, as well as on the man in the street."—*Leeds Mercury.*

"His interesting text is accompanied by numerous illustrations, many of them full-page, and altogether his book is one which has every claim to a warm welcome from those who have a taste for ecclesiastical archæology."—*Glasgow Herald.*

"This is an interesting and descriptive account of the various churches still extant in London, and is illustrated by several excellent photographs. . . . His work will be of value to the antiquarian, and of interest to the casual observer."—*Western Morning News.*

"Mr. Daniell's work will prove very interesting reading, as he has evidently taken great care in obtaining all the facts concerning the City churches, their history and associations."—*London.*

"The illustrations to this book are good, and it deserves to be widely read."—*Morning Post.*

ARCHIBALD CONSTABLE & CO
2 WHITEHALL GARDENS WESTMINSTER

Crown 8vo, 3s. 6d.

The Shoulder of Shasta

By BRAM STOKER

Author of " Dracula."

" Will be one of the most popular romances, in one volume, of the season now opening. It is chiefly remarkable for the very marked and superior descriptive power displayed by the author in his rich and inspiring picture of the scenery of the Shasta Mountain. . . . So entirely unconventional, humorous, and bizarre, as to be quite unique. . . . The composition is bold and lucid. . . . He is an accomplished artist, and shows here at his best. . . . Mr. Bram Stoker will add widely to his reputation by this."—*Irish Times.*

" A pure and well-told story."—*Glasgow Herald.*

" The story is charmingly written, and deserves to be read for its brilliant open-air passages, and the portrait it contains of Grizzly Dick."—*Daily News.*

" Mr. Bram Stoker has given the reading world one of the breeziest and most picturesque tales of life on the Pacific slope that has been penned for many a long day."—*Daily Telegraph.*

" Mr. Stoker seems quite at home in picturing the wild beauty of Californian scenery. . . . 'The Shoulder of Shasta' is eminently fresh and readable."—*Globe.*

" It is a capital story."—*Bristol Times and Mirror.*

" The story is gracefully conceived, and wrought out with considerable skill. . . . A readable and entertaining work."—*Scotsman.*

" 'The Shoulder of Shasta' may fairly be classed among the books to be read and enjoyed."—*Yorkshire Post.*

" A pleasant story of life in Western America. . . . Fresh and unconventional."—*Publishers' Circular.*

" Mr. Bram Stoker's new book is a peculiarly bright and breezy story of Californian life. . . . There is nothing laboured in this description, no straining after undue effect. . . . The language is simple, yet the effect is always satisfying, and the word-picture is complete."—*Liverpool Daily Post.*

" The narrative is entertaining throughout, with eloquent descriptions of scenery."—*Academy.*

" Mr. Bram Stoker's story is unflagging, full of vigour, and capital reading from end to end ; moreover, it conveys a vivid picture of life and manners in a corner of the world better known to him than to the majority of those who will read his book."—*Standard.*

The Fortune of a Spendthrift

AND OTHER ITEMS

By R. ANDOM

Author of " We Three and Troddles," " The Strange Adventures of Roger Wilkins," etc., etc.

AND

FRED HAREWOOD

" Lightly, briskly, and pleasantly written."—*Scotsman.*

" The adventures of a spendthrift, which form the principal feature of the book, are related with so much dramatic force that any improbabilities of the plot are forgotten in the reader's eagerness to learn the *dénouement*. . . . Treated with freshness in a pleasant, graphic style, and a lively interest is cleverly sustained. . . . They are all told with spirit and vivacity, and show no little skill in their descriptive passages."—*Literary World.*

" A collection of brightly-written short stories, well adapted for a holiday afternoon."—*Globe.*

ARCHIBALD CONSTABLE & CO

2 WHITEHALL GARDENS WESTMINSTER

Hans van Donder

A Romance of Boer Life.

By CHARLES MONTAGUE, Author of "The Vigil."

Fcap. 8vo, 2s. 6d.

"Mr. Montague has written another charming romance."—*Scotsman.*
"Admirably told. The descriptions of Big Game Shooting are highly exciting."—*Glasgow Herald.*

Torriba   By JOHN CAMERON GRANT.

Fcap. 8vo, 2s. 6d.

"Torriba is unquestionably bold in treatment and well written."—*Globe.*

Madge o' the Pool   By WILLIAM SHARP.

Fcap. 8vo, 2s. 6d.

"Excellent."—*Athenæum.*

A Writer of Fiction   A Novel.

By CLIVE HOLLAND,

Author of "My Japanese Wife." *Cloth extra, 2s. 6d.*

"Intensely interesting."—*Glasgow Daily Mail.*
"A striking story."—*Pall Mall Gazette.*

The Love of an Obsolete Woman

CHRONICLED BY HERSELF.

2s. 6d.

"A fascinating book. True to life and highly artistic."—*Publishers' Circular.*

Angela's Lover   BY DOROTHEA GERARD

Paper, 1s. Cloth extra, 2s.

"Charming."—*Scotsman.*

A Full Confession   BY F. C. PHILLIPS

1s. net.

"In brief—direct and forcible."—*Literary World.*

The Parasite   BY CONAN DOYLE

1s. net.

ARCHIBALD CONSTABLE & CO
2 WHITEHALL GARDENS WESTMINSTER

" The Game of Polo "

By T. F. DALE

(" Stoneclink " of " The Field ")

Illustrated by LILLIAN SMYTHE, CUTHBERT BRADLEY, and CRAWFORD WOOD ; and a Photogravure Portrait of Mr. JOHN WATSON.

Demy 8vo. One Guinea net.

" Likely to rank as the standard work on the subject."—*Morning Post.*
" What the author does not know about it is not knowledge."—*Pall Mall Gazette.*
" Will doubtless be of great use to beginners."—*Illustrated Sporting and Dramatic.*
" A charming addition to the library of those who are devoted to the game."—*The Globe.*

The Art and Pastime of Cycling

By R. J. MACREDY AND A. J. WILSON

New Edition, and in a large measure rewritten. Profusely illustrated

Cloth, 1s. 6d. Paper Cover, 1s.

" One of the most complete books on Cycling—deals with every phase of the noble Sport."—*Cycle and Camera.*
" An eminently useful handbook."—*South Africa.*
" Full of information."—*Scotsman.*
" A great fund of useful and practical information."—*The Field.*
"The Fourth Edition of this book, and better than ever. . . . No cyclist's library is complete without it."—*Bicycling News.*

With Plumer in Matabeleland

By FRANK W. SYKES

With numerous Illustrations in the text, and 35 Full-page Plates and Two Maps. Demy 8vo, 15s. net.

" Operations of the Force during the Rebellion of 1896 are described in great detail, and in a very interesting fashion."—*Financial Times.*
" Mr. Sykes served as a trooper in the M.R.F., and depicts with much point and piquancy the life of the rank and file of that corps as it presented itself to him throughout the campaign. Still more delightful is the racy vein in which the humours of the situation are recounted. Mr. Sykes' narrative of ' Massacres and Escapes' is a noble record. Many incidents not hitherto mentioned of pluck and heroism are alluded to. *His book is one of the best of its class we have yet had the pleasure of reviewing*."—*South Africa.*
"The chapter on the Religion of the Matabele is well worth reading, so from first page to last is Mr. Sykes' book."—*Daily News.*
" The best illustrated and most generally interesting volume. . . . Frank, catholic, fearless, and generous. I congratulate him, and also his assistants on a notable volume."—*African Critic.*

Imperial Defence

By Sir CHARLES DILKE and SPENSER WILKINSON

New and Revised Edition. 2s. 6d.

" To urge our countrymen to prepare, whilst there is yet time, for a defence that is required alike by interest, honour, and duty, and by the best traditions of the nation's history."—*Daily Mail.*

ARCHIBALD CONSTABLE & CO

2 WHITEHALL GARDENS WESTMINSTER

The Paston Letters,

1422–1509

EDITED BY JAMES GAIRDNER

OF THE PUBLIC RECORD OFFICE

3 Vols. Fcap. 8vo. With 3 Photogravure Frontispieces, cloth gilt extra, or paper label uncut, 16s. net.

These letters are the genuine correspondence of a family in Norfolk during the Wars of the Roses. As such, they are altogether unique in character ; yet the language is not so antiquated as to present any serious difficulty to the modern reader. The topics of the letters relate partly to the private affairs of the family, and partly to the stirring events of the time : and the correspondence includes State papers, love letters, bailiff's accounts, sentimental poems, jocular epistles, etc.

" This edition, which was first published some twenty years ago, is the standard edition of these remarkable historical documents, and contains upward of four hundred letters in addition to those published by Frere in 1823. The reprint is in three small and compact volumes, and should be welcome to students of history as giving an important work in a convenient form."—*Scotsman.*

"Unquestionably the standard edition of these curious literary relics of an age so long ago that the writers speak of the battles between the contending forces of York and Lancaster as occurrences of the moment."—*Daily News.*

" One of the monuments of English historical scholarship that needs no commendation."—*Manchester Guardian.*

ARCHIBALD CONSTABLE & CO
2 WHITEHALL GARDENS WESTMINSTER

Boswell's Life of Johnson

EDITED BY AUGUSTINE BIRRELL.

WITH FRONTISPIECES BY ALEX ANSTED, A REPRODUCTION OF SIR JOSHUA REYNOLDS' PORTRAIT.

Six Volumes. Foolscap 8vo. Cloth, paper label, or gilt extra, 2s. net per Volume. Also half morocco, 3s. net per Volume. Sold in Sets only.

In 48 Volumes

CONSTABLE'S REPRINT

OF

The Waverley Novels

THE FAVOURITE EDITION OF

SIR WALTER SCOTT.

With all the original Plates and Vignettes (Re-engraved). In 48 Vols.

Foolscap 8vo. Cloth, paper label title, 1s. 6d. net per Volume, or £3 12s. the Set. Also cloth gilt, gilt top, 2s. net per Volume, or £4 16s. the Set ; and half leather gilt, 2s. 6d. net per Volume, or £6 the Set.

ARCHIBALD CONSTABLE & CO

2 WHITEHALL GARDENS WESTMINSTER

The Nation's Awakening

By SPENSER WILKINSON

Crown 8vo, 3s. 6d.

"The essence of true policy for Britain, the policy of common-sense, lies, according to Mr. Wilkinson, in choosing for assertion and for active defence those points in the extensive fringe of our world-wide interests, and those moments of time at which our self-defence will coincide with the self-defence of the world. This idea he works out in a clever and vigorous fashion."—*Glasgow Herald.*

"He elaborates his views in four 'books,' dealing respectively with the aims of the other Great Powers, the defence of British interests, the organization of the Government, and 'the idea of the nation,' . . . he deprecates a policy of isolation, and advocates a closer alliance with Germany."—*Scotsman.*

"We consider Mr. Wilkinson completely proves his case. We agree . . . that Mr. Spenser Wilkinson must make all men think. We welcome the volume, as we have welcomed previous volumes from Mr. Wilkinson's pen, as of the highest value towards the formation of a national policy, of which we never stood in greater need."—*Athenæum.*

"These essays show a wide knowledge of international politics."—*Morning Post.*

BY THE SAME AUTHOR

The Volunteers and the National Defence
Crown 8vo, cloth, 2s. 6d.

The Brain of an Army
Crown 8vo, cloth, 2s. 6d.

The Command of the Sea
Crown 8vo, paper, 1s.

The Brain of the Navy
Crown 8vo, paper, 1s.

ARCHIBALD CONSTABLE & CO
2 WHITEHALL GARDENS WESTMINSTER

CONSTABLE'S
Hand Atlas of India

A NEW SERIES of Sixty Maps and Plans
prepared from Ordnance and other Surveys
under the direction of

J. G. BARTHOLOMEW, F.R.G.S., ·F.R.S.E., &c.

In half morocco, or full bound cloth, gilt top, 14s.

This Atlas is the first publication of its kind, and for tourists and travellers generally it will be found particularly useful. There are Twenty-two Plans of the principal towns of our Indian Empire, based on the most recent surveys, and officially revised to date in India.

The Topographical Section Maps are an accurate reduction of the Survey of India, and contain all the places described in Sir W. W. Hunter's "Gazetteer of India," according to his spelling.

The Military, Railway, Telegraph, and Mission Station Maps are designed to meet the requirements of the Military and Civil Service, also missionaries and business men who at present have no means of obtaining the information they require in a handy form.

The index contains upwards of ten thousand names, and will be found more complete than any yet attempted on a similar scale.

Further to increase the utility of the work as a reference volume, an abstract of the 1891 Census has been added.

"It is tolerably safe to predict that no sensible traveller will go to India in future without providing himself with 'Constable's Hand Atlas of India.' Nothing half so useful has been done for many years to help both the traveller in India and the student at home. 'Constable's Hand Atlas' is a pleasure to hold and to turn over."—*Athenæum.*

ARCHIBALD CONSTABLE & CO
2 WHITEHALL GARDENS WESTMINSTER

www.ingramcontent.com/pod-product-compliance
Lightning Source LLC
Chambersburg PA
CBHW020606030726
47497CB00007B/2107